# JY YANG

# THE RED THREADS
# OF FORTUNE

A TOM DOHERTY ASSOCIATES BOOK

NEW YORK

This is a work of fiction. All of the characters, organizations, and events portrayed in this novella are either products of the author's imagination or are used fictitiously.

Cover illustration by Yuko Shimizu
Cover design by Christine Foltzer

Map by Serena Maylon

Edited by Carl Engle-Laird

A Tor.com Book
Published by Tom Doherty Associates
175 Fifth Avenue
New York, NY 10010

www.tor.com

Tor® is a registered trademark of
Macmillan Publishing Group, LLC.

ISBN 978-0-7653-9538-2 (ebook)
ISBN 978-0-7653-9539-9 (trade paperback)

*For the dangerous hearts that kept me going*

GREAT STORMS

ENDLESS SEAS

GUSAI
DESERT

BATANAAR

x.

xv.

GAUR
ANTAM

VISHARAN

vi.

TIGUMAN

ix.

NAM
MIN

xi.

MATAPUR

ATHARAYABAD

viii.

EL ZAHARAD

THIEN CHIH

THE FIRE
ISLANDS

DEMONS' OCEAN

THE QUARTERLANDS

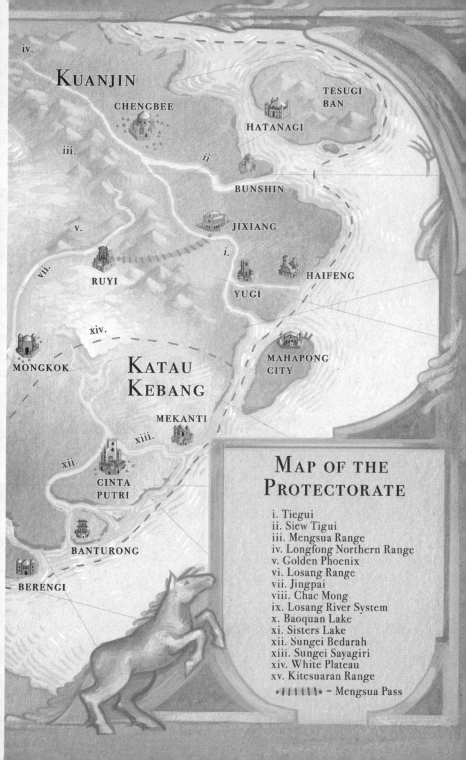

iv.

# KUANJIN

CHENGBEE

TESUGI BAN

HATANAGI

iii.

ii.

BUNSHIN

JIXIANG

v.

i.

vii.

RUYI

HAIFENG

YUGI

xiv.

# KATAU KEBANG

MONGKOK

MAHAPONG CITY

MEKANTI

xiii.

xii.

CINTA PUTRI

BANTURONG

BERENGI

## MAP OF THE PROTECTORATE

i. Tiegui
ii. Siew Tigui
iii. Mengsua Range
iv. Longfong Northern Range
v. Golden Phoenix
vi. Losang Range
vii. Jingpai
viii. Chac Mong
ix. Losang River System
x. Baoquan Lake
xi. Sisters Lake
xii. Sungei Bedarah
xiii. Sungei Sayagiri
xiv. White Plateau
xv. Kitesuaran Range

•⌇⌇⌇⌇⌇⌇• = Mengsua Pass

# Acknowledgments

Writing this novella was an adventure. I think I completely overhauled it three times at least—and once at a very late stage after it had already been line edited, much to the chagrin of my editor.

So first thanks go to my very patient and much put-upon editor, Carl Engle-Laird. Not just for taking a chance on this generally unknown short story writer and inviting me to send him something, but also for sticking with me even as I cost him (probably) many sleepless nights. You're awesome.

Irene Gallo, Christine Foltzer, and Yuko Shimizu conspired to give the novellas some of the most handsome covers I have ever seen. Months later, I'm still gobsmacked. Many, many thanks for making the books as gorgeous as they are.

A whole slew of people saw this book at various points in its larval development and offered critique. My gratitude toward Amit Chaudhuri, Nino Cipri, Kate Elliot, Georgina Kamsika, S. Qiouyi Lu, Jean McNeil, Nicasio Reed, Bogi Takács, Jay Wolf, and Isabel Yap: this book is what it is because of you.

Special thanks goes to Grace P. Fong for doing the wonderful artwork that accompanied the announcement of the novellas, in record time. Did I ever tell you that you're amazing? Because you are.

Finally, I could not have done all of this without the help of my superagent, DongWon. Thank you so much for believing in my work and always having my back.

# PART ONE

# RIDER

# Chapter One

**KILLING THE VOICE TRANSMITTER** was an overreaction. Even Mokoya knew that.

Half a second after she had crushed the palm-sized device to a pulp of sparking, smoking metal, she found herself frantically tensing through water-nature, trying to undo the fatal blow. Crumpled steel groaned as she reversed her actions, using the Slack to pull instead of push. The transmitter unfolded, opening up like a spring blossom, but it was no use. The machine was a complex thing, and like all complex things, it was despairingly hard to fix once broken.

Mokoya might have stood a chance with a Tensor's invention, anything that relied on knots of slackcraft to manipulate objects in the material world. But this was a Machinist device. It worked on physical principles Mokoya had never learned and did not understand. Its shattered innards were a foreign language of torn wires and pulverized magnets. The transmitter lay dead on her wrist, Adi's strident voice never to squawk forth from it again.

"Cheebye," she swore. *"Cheebye."*

Mokoya repeated the expletive a third time, then a fourth and a fifth and a sixth, head bowed prayerfully over the transmitter's corpse as she swayed on her mount. Phoenix breathed patiently, massive rib cage expanding and deflating, while her rider recited swearwords until her heart stopped stuttering.

The desert wind howled overhead.

Finally Mokoya straightened up. Around her, the Gusai desert had been simplified to macrogeology by the moonlight: dunes and rock behind, canyon and cave in front. A thread of the Copper Oasis shone in the overlapping valleys before her. Sky and sand were blissfully, thankfully empty from horizon to horizon.

No naga. And if the fortunes were kind, she would not meet one before she returned to camp.

Scouting alone was a mistake. Mokoya knew that. The crew had followed a scattered, crooked trail of dead animals and spoor for a dozen sun-cycles, and it had brought them here. Experience told them that the naga's nest would be hidden in the canyon, with its warren of caverns carved out through the ages. The chance of a scouting party crossing paths with the beast while it hunted during the sundown hours was very real.

And yet Mokoya had convinced Adi to let her take Phoenix and the raptor pack to explore the sands east of the camp by herself. *I'm a Tensor,* she had said. *I trained as a pugilist in the Grand Monastery. I can handle a naga, no matter how big. I'm the only one on this crew who can.*

Unbelievably, she had said, *I know what I'm doing. I'm not a madwoman.*

Just as unbelievably, Adi had let her go. She had grumbled, "Ha nah ha nah, you go lah, not my pasal whether you die or not," but her expression plainly said she was doing this to prevent more quarreling and that she considered this a favor to Mokoya, one she intended to collect on. And so Mokoya had escaped into the cool darkness, the open sands imposing no small talk or judgment or obligation, free of all the things that might trigger her temper.

Now, barely an hour later, she had already destroyed the transmitter entrusted to her care. Even if she avoided encountering the naga, she still had to explain the transmitter's death.

She had no good excuses. She could lie and say it was done in anger, because Adi would not stop fucking calling to check whether she was still alive. But such violence was the hallmark of a petty and unstable woman, instead of a Tensor in full control of her faculties.

And what of the truth? Could she admit she had been startled by Adi's voice coming out of nowhere and had lashed out like a frightened animal?

No. Focus. This question could be answered later.

Getting distracted by these neurotic detours had allowed shimmering pressure to sneak back into her chest. Mokoya shook her head, as if she could dislodge the unwanted thoughts and emotions.

Phoenix sympathetically swayed her massive head. Her head feathers rustled like a grass skirt. Perched on the giant raptor's back, Mokoya cooed and petted her as though she weren't a beast the size of a house, but a small child. Phoenix was a gentle, happy creature, but one wouldn't know it just looking at her. In cities, people scattered at her approach. Sometimes the scattering was accompanied by screaming. And sometimes Phoenix would think it was a game and chase them.

Mokoya avoided cities these days.

A hooting noise heralded the return of her raptor pack. A hundred yields ahead of Phoenix, the flat sandy ground dropped away and folded into a crevasse: the beginning of the steep, scrub-encrusted canyon that bordered the Copper Oasis. It was over this lip that Mokoya had sent the eight raptors on their hunt for quarry. They were really Adi's raptors, raised by the royal houses of Katau Kebang in the far south of the Protectorate's reach and trained in the arts of hunting any naga that strayed across the Demons' Ocean.

The first leapt into view and landed in a cloud of sand, tail held like a rudder for balance, teeth and claws splendid in the moonlight. They were exactly like Phoenix—narrow-headed, long-limbed, plumed in coruscating feathers—only differing in size (and in other aspects that Mokoya did not like to discuss). One by one they loped toward their giant sister and stood patiently at attention, their hot breaths a whistling symphony.

Nothing. The raptors had found nothing.

Mokoya's fingers tightened around Phoenix's reins. If she listened to common sense, it would tell her to return to camp immediately. It would tell her that lingering alone in a naga's territory with a dead communications device was tempting the fortunes. It would tell her that there were worse things in this forsaken world than having to fend off Adi's wrath, as if she didn't already know.

She whistled and sent the raptors farther east to comb through more of the valley.

As Phoenix slouched after the sprightly creatures, her clawed feet sinking deep into the sand, the weight of the dead transmitter pulled on Mokoya's left wrist, reminding her what a fool she was. Mokoya ignored it and reasoned with herself, running guilt-assuaging lines of thought through her head. This assignment was an abnormal one, and abnormal circumstances called for abnormal tactics. She was making the right move, plowing through unturned ground as fast as she could.

The sooner she found the naga's gravesent nest, the

sooner they could get out of this blighted desert with its parched winds that could peel skin and blind the unwary. And that was the sooner Mokoya could get away from Bataanar and its web of things she did not want to get tangled up in.

Naga hunting was a specialty of Adi's crew. In the uncharted south past the Demons' Ocean lay the Quarterlands with their permissive half gravity, separated from the Protectorate by the claws of sea tempests that no ship with hoisted sails could cross. Megafauna lived there: crocodiles the size of ships, sloths the size of horses, horses the size of houses.

Above all, there were the naga. More lizard than serpent, they soared through the skies on wings of leather, bird boned and jewel toned. These were apex predators, graceful and deadly, inscribed into the journals of adventurers with the kind of reverence reserved for the gods of old. A single bite could cut a man in half.

But even gods had limits. When the storm winds caught unwary naga and tossed them across the Demons' Ocean, they turned ugly and ravenous, struggling against the newfound heaviness of their bodies. Full gravity ravaged them, sucked them dry of energy, turned their predator's hunger into a scything force of destruction. Mokoya had seen countrysides decimated and villages torn to shreds as they attacked and devoured anything that moved. The crew ran capture-and-release operations whenever they could, but over the two years Mokoya had worked for Adi, through dozens and dozens of cases, only twice had the naga been allowed to live.

And *yet*. The stupidity of humankind knew no bounds. Calls north of Jixiang meant an escaped pet, scarred by chains and fear. Smuggled eggs, hunting trophies, bribes from Quarterlandish merchants: the wealthy and privileged had many means of sating their lust for conquering the unknown. Naga raised in full gravity grew up malformed and angry, racked by constant pain, intractable once they had broken their bonds. Adi said that killing these creatures was a mercy. Mokoya thought it should have been the owners who were strung up.

Then there was this case. The Gusai desert lay in the high north, on the edge of the Protectorate's influence. There was nothing out here except hematite mines and a city to house the miners in: Bataanar. The naga they hunted hadn't come from here. The trail of reported sightings, breathless and disjointed, pointed a straight line toward the capital city, Chengbee. Between Bataanar and Chengbee stood a thousand li of mountains and barren wilderness, two days' travel for even the most determined flyer. And wild naga hunted in spirals, not straight lines. Straight lines were the precinct of creatures that knew their destination.

That was the first abnormality. The second was the naga's size. From the mouths of frightened citizens came reports of a beast three, six, ten times larger than anything they'd ever seen. One exaggeration could be excused by hyperbole, three could be explained as a pattern induced by fear, but two dozen meant some form of truth was buried in them. So—the creature was big, even for a naga. That implied it wasn't a wild capture, that something had been done to the beast.

The third abnormality wasn't about the naga. It was Bataanar itself. An ordinary citizen might consider it a humble mining city of a few thousand workers, watched over by a dozen Protectorate Tensors and the raja, who was answerable to the Protector. A *Machinist* would know that Mokoya's twin brother, Akeha, had turned the city into a base for the movement, a nerve center of the rebellion far from the Protectorate's influence. And an ordinary Tensor might not know anything about the tremors of power that rumbled under the foundations of the city, but a *well-placed* one would know that Raja Ponchak, the first raja of the city, had passed two years ago. And while Ponchak had been a Machinist sympathizer, her husband, Choonghey—the new raja in her stead—was not. Bataanar was a recipe for disaster, on the cusp of boiling over.

The fourth abnormality was not, in fact, an abnormality, but merely a rumor. A rumor of Tensor experiments in the capital: whispers about a group who had taken animals and grafted knots of Slack-connections—like human souls—onto their physical existences. The details of these rumors sent uncomfortable shivers of familiarity through Mokoya. She felt somehow culpable.

Putting these four things together, one could only guess that the naga they hunted was one of these unfortunate experiments, sent by the Protectorate to destroy Bataanar and cripple the Machinist rebellion. The fact that the creature was skulking around and killing desert rodents for sustenance lent credence to the idea that someone was controlling it. It was *waiting* for something.

Abnormal circumstances, Mokoya reminded herself. Abnormal tactics. She was being perfectly rational. Adi would agree with her on this. Or maybe Adi wouldn't. But Akeha would, her brother would, he would understand. Or Yongcheow. Or—

Mokoya exhaled shakily. Now was not the time. She had drifted from the present again. Pay attention. Focus on Phoenix, patient and rumbling under her. On the sand bluff the raptors had disappeared over. Focus on breathing.

Something was wrong. Her right arm hurt. An ache ran from the tip of her scale-sheathed fingers to the knitted edge of her shoulder, where the grafted skin yielded to scar tissue. Spun from lizardflesh, her arm called naga blood through the forest-nature of the Slack. Was the beast close by? Mokoya clenched her right hand. Tendons emerged in pebbled skin turned yellow by stress, but it didn't help.

She raised the hand into view, splaying the fingers like a stretching cat. Tremors ran through them. "Cheebye," she hissed at herself, as if she could swear herself into calmness.

Perhaps profanity was not the answer. Mokoya wet cracked lips and closed her eyes. Her mindeye expanded, the world turning into wrinkled cloth, each bump and fold representing an object. On top of that, like colored paper over a lantern, lay the Slack with its five natures.

There she was: Sanao Mokoya, a blaze of light spreading outward, a concentrated ball of connections to the Slack. Still human, despite everything. Under her was Phoenix, with her peculiar condition, unnatural brilliance garlanding her body. The raptor's massive bulk warped the fabric of the Slack. Farther out, over the cliff edge, raced the pinpoints of the raptors, tiny ripples in the Slack, running toward her—

Wait. Why were they coming back?

Mokoya's eyes flew open just as Phoenix barked in

fear. She barely had time to seize the reins before her mount spun in the sand. "Phoenix—" she gasped.

The raptors burst over the bluff like a storm wave, chittering war cries.

A wall of air hit her from behind.

Moon and stars vanished. Phoenix reared, and Mokoya lost her grip. She fell. In the second between the lurch of her stomach and her back hitting the sand, there was a glimpse of sky, and this is what she saw: an eclipse of scaly white belly, wings stretched from end to end, red-veined skin webbed between spindly fingers.

*Naga sun-chaser. Naga sun-eater.*

Hitting ground knocked the wind out of Mokoya, but she had no time to register pain. The naga beat its wings, and sand leapt into her nose and mouth. The creature soared over the valley, long tail trailing after it.

Braying, Phoenix sprinted toward the canyon drop. The raptor pack followed.

"Phoenix!" Mokoya scrambled up, knees and ankles fighting the soft sand. Her reflexes struck; she tensed through water-nature and threw a force-barrier across the razor line of desert bluff. Nausea juddered through her as Phoenix bounced off the barrier, safe for now. Safe. The raptor pack formed a barking chorus along the edge.

As though a thick layer of glass stood between her and the world, Mokoya watched the shape of the naga descend into the canyon toward the caverns nestled within the far wall. Wings bigger than ships' sails, barbed tail like a whip, horned and whiskered head bedecked with iridescent scales. Creatures of that size turned mythical from a distance. Nothing living should have the gall to compete with cliff and mountain.

The naga spiraled downward and was swallowed by shadow, vanishing into valley fold and cavern roof. Gasping, Mokoya released her hold on water-nature, and the barrier across the sand bluff dissolved into nothing.

She sank to her knees, forehead collapsing against the cool sands. Great Slack. Great Slack. She was lucky to be alive. She was lucky to—It should have killed her. Maybe it wasn't hungry. It could have picked Phoenix off. It could have—

Her heart struggled to maintain its rhythm. How had she missed it? This shouldn't have happened. Even as a juvenile, a naga's bulk had enough pull to deform the Slack, stretching it like a sugar-spinner's thread. She should have felt it coming. She hadn't. She had been too distracted.

"Cheebye," she whispered. "Cheebye."

Her nerves were trying to suffocate her. This was pathetic. She was Sanao Mokoya. Daughter of the Protector, ex-prophet, former instigator of rebellion in the heart of the capital. She had passed through hellfire and survived. What was all her training for, all those years of honing her discipline, if the smallest, stupidest things—like a quarrel with her brother, for example—could bring her to ruin?

Still kneeling, she kept her eyes shut and moved her lips through a calming recitation. A last-resort tactic. The words she muttered were so familiar to her, they had been bleached of all meaning.

*Remember you, bright seeker of knowledge, the First Sutra, the Sutra of Five Natures.*

*The Slack is all, and all is the Slack.*

*It knows no beginning and no end, no time and no space.*

*All that is, exists through the grace of the Slack. All that moves, moves through the grace of the Slack.*

*The firmament is divided into the five natures of the Slack, and in them is written all the ways of things and the natural world.*

*First is the nature of earth. Know it through the weight of mountains and stone, the nature of things when they are at rest.*

*Second is the nature of water. Know it through the strength of storms and rivers, the nature of things that are in motion.*

*Third is the nature of fire. Know it through the rising of air and the melt of winter ice, the nature of things that gives them their temperature.*

*Fourth is the nature of forests. Know it through the beat*

*of your heart and the warmth of your blood, the nature of things that grow and live.*

*Fifth is the nature of metal. Know it through the speed of lightning and the pull of iron, the nature of things that spark and attract.*

*Know the ways of the five natures, and you will know the ways of the world. For the lines and knots of the Slack are the lines and knots of the world, and all that is shaped is shaped through the twining of the red threads of fortune.*

It was a long spiel. So long that by the time her attention had slogged all the way to its odious end, her lungs had stopped trying to collapse upon themselves. Her head still hurt, lines of stress running from the crown to the joints of neck and shoulder, but her legs held when she stood.

Phoenix came and pressed her massive snout against Mokoya, whining in distress. "Shh," Mokoya said, palms gentle against the pebbled skin of the creature's nose. "Everything will be okay. I'm here. Nothing can hurt you."

The raptor pack circled them. They were almost as tall as Mokoya when dismounted. Unlike her, they seemed to be largely unaffected by the naga's passage.

Mokoya marked the spot where the beast had disappeared. She could spin this into a triumph. No more hunting, no more groping through unsympathetic desert searching for signs. She had found the naga's nest. And the best part of it: defying the reports they'd heard, the naga was *average* for its kind. They'd hunted bigger; they'd certainly captured bigger. This wasn't the other-worldly monstrosity Mokoya had been fearing. Adi's crew could definitely handle this one without problems.

Mokoya raised her left wrist to deliver the good news, then remembered what she'd done to the transmitter. *Cheebye.*

Wait. No. There was still the talker. How could she have forgotten?

Phoenix lowered herself to the sand at Mokoya's command. She reached into the saddlebag and rooted around until she collided with the talker's small round mass, the bronze hard and warm against her palm. Tensing through metal-nature infused the object with life-giving electricity. Its geometric lines lit up, plates separating into a loose sphere. Slackcraft. Mokoya turned the plates until they formed the configuration twinned with Adi's talker.

Several seconds passed. Adi's voice welled up from the glowing sphere. "Mokoya! Kanina—is that you or a ghost?"

"It's me, Adi. I'm not dead yet."

An annoyed noise, another expletive. "Eh, hello, I let you go by yourself doesn't mean you can ignore me, okay? What happened to Yongcheow's stupid machine?"

"Something," Mokoya demurred. "An accident." She leaned against Phoenix's warm, patient bulk. Get to the point. "Adi, I'm coming back. I found the nest. I did it, all right? I found the naga's nest."

# Chapter Two

**THE VISION HIT MOKOYA** on the way back to camp.

As usual, the warning signs came too late. Dizziness, a shot of vertigo, and frisson up the spine. Not enough time to dismount and get to stable ground before the Slack punched her into the past, soup-heavy and pungent.

The world snapped into a different form. Sunfall-sky, tang of firecracker smoke, crash of trumpets and drums. Mokoya was eight years old, brimming with anxiety as she shivered on the upper floor of an inn over a choreographed riot of color and noise. The spring procession. Chengbee. Behind her was Master Sung, Head Abbot of the Grand Monastery, and twenty pugilists he had handpicked. All of them scanned the sky, waiting for it to betray the first hint of horned head, of wings swallowing the falling sun.

Two weeks before, Mokoya had had a nightmare of celebration shredded by death. It was a desperately specific nightmare, of the sort that Mokoya had been plagued with recently. The sort that then came to pass exactly as Mokoya had seen them.

If this nightmare was like the others, it meant a naga would attack the spring procession when the sun fell. She did not want it to. She did not want to be labeled a prophet, someone who saw the future in dreams. She did not know why it was happening to her.

Beside her stood Akeha. Her twin, her anchor. In this time before they had confirmed their genders, she was his mirror, and they were indistinguishable except for her mismatched eyes. He let the sides of their hands touch, to show that he wasn't afraid. He wasn't afraid of her.

The sky deepened rapidly to plum, then bruise-black. Sunfall.

Everything tumbled forward with terrifying speed. Darkness descended, deeper than twilight. The awning of a naga's wings blanketed the horizon: someone's trophy pet, frightened and angry. The crowd screamed, and the pugilists kicked off, rising in a cloud, weapons primed and humming.

But it was Akeha, bright Akeha, who moved fastest. He closed his fist over his head, and water-nature surged. An animal scream split the air. The naga's massive body twisted, plunging in free fall. Someone grabbed her shoulder. Someone shouted, "Jump!" Mokoya leapt forward, and—

She was lying on her back, sand clotting her mouth

and burning her eyes. Confusion, at first, then clarity. Her name was Sanao Mokoya, she was thirty-nine years old, and she was no longer a prophet. In exchange for grim futures, she had gained a lizard arm and a mass of scars congealed across her face and body. This was the Gusai desert. She did not fear naga. She hunted them.

Phoenix lay next to her on the sand, an obedient mound of raptor, breath disturbing the red sands. Slowly Mokoya sat up, ignoring the pain that flared through her hip. Bodily pain was a temporary condition. She knew this.

Lashed to her waist was the dream recorder she always wore, a box of intricately carved bronze bearing the heavy patina of age and the particular workmanship of the Protector's court. Powered by slackcraft, it had been a constant presence in her life since childhood, when the adults around her had wanted records of every Slack-touched vision.

The box hummed with another successful dream capture, a satisfied sound that was almost gleeful.

Mokoya flipped its lid and extracted its contents: a palm-sized glass pearl, teardrop-shaped and freshly filled, insides swirling with opalescent colors. Not liquid, just light, an imprinted pattern in the Slack.

Once upon a time, when she still saw the future in dreams, each filled capture pearl would be taken by

Tensors and analyzed over and over, every drop of meaning and context wrung from its innards.

Then the accident happened, and the gift of prophecy left her. When the Slack hit her these days, it was with moments from her past, even ones she herself had forgotten. Her dream recorder, ever faithful, caught these fragments of history in its glass droplets.

Sometimes they were useful. In Phoenix's saddlebag, nestled amongst the thick folds of brocade, lay a dozen other capture pearls, their bellies full of slivers from happier times. Gap-toothed smiles, sticky fingers, a little girl's hair haloed in summer light. But sometimes it was moments like these, full of things she didn't care to remember.

Mokoya twisted the capture pearl in her hands. Up to that point in their lives, she and Akeha had been ordinary children, sold by the Protector to the Grand Monastery to repay a debt, content to live their lives in ascetic obscurity. After Mokoya had been confirmed a prophet, their lives had started the thirty-year-long process of coming apart. Why would she want to keep something like that?

She tensed the vision out of the pearl, unknotting the braids in the Slack that kept it in existence. Briefly a thought crossed her mind: she should undo the skin on her wrists and belly, and spill her blood and guts into the soft sand. Let her flesh be dissolved by the wind and her bones be bleached by the sun.

Mokoya looked at Phoenix. The raptor huffed, patiently waiting for her to move on.

With a sigh, Mokoya got to her feet. She felt calmer now, or at least numb, as though the vision had lanced through her chest and drained the abscess of nervous energy. "Come," she said to Phoenix. "Let's get going."

~

"We should capture it."

Yongcheow and Adi exchanged a glance. One was the willowy Tensor son of a magistrate, raised among silk and baubles; the other a simple Kebangilan herder woman, squat and ropy from years of hard work. But the language their eyes spoke was universal.

"You gila or what?" Adi asked with a squint.

"I'm *not* a madwoman," Mokoya said, and this time her conviction was real. "I'm telling you, I saw the naga with my own two eyes. We can handle it. Why would I lie to you?"

"Because you have *completely* lost your mind," Yongcheow snapped, arms hedged across his chest. The loss of his transmitter stung, and he was in no mood to play nice with his sister-in-law. Akeha had sent him with the crew to keep an eye on things, but everyone knew it was really to keep an eye on Mokoya, and the two had scratched at each other's nerves for a dozen sun-cycles.

Mokoya was tired. She ignored him and looked at Adi. As crew captain, her decision was the only one that mattered. "This will be no different from any other assignment," she said. "We know where the naga is *now*. If we wait for the Machinists to tell us what to do, we might lose it. It might move on. Or attack. We can't delay." She added, more amicably, "You're not the delaying kind."

"No meh?" Adi's face bore skepticism, but Mokoya could see her resistance crumbling like weathered clay. She was a practical person, after all, someone whose world was structured to avoid the stingers and thorns of politics. Born a princess to a sprawling, squabbling family, she had married a commoner to escape the strictures of royal life, only to divorce him later. Adi was a woman of few regrets. This assignment—which she had agreed to for Mokoya's sake—might be one of them.

It was a sentiment Mokoya shared.

Yongcheow scowled. "Look, I know you think I know nothing. Fine. Will you at least listen to the wisdom of the Machinists? This is no ordinary naga, blown from the Quarterlands by accident. The Tensors did something to it. The Protectorate sent it here for a reason. We can't treat this like one of your normal hunts."

Mokoya said, "The Machinists' report said the naga

was big. It's not. Obviously their wisdom has large gaps."

A frustrated burst of air escaped Yongcheow. "The pugilists from the Grand Monastery arrive tomorrow. Let's at least wait until—"

Mokoya snapped, "We don't need Thennjay's help."

Silence buried them all. In the heartbeats that followed, Mokoya knew she had spoken too loudly, too fiercely, and cursed the looseness of her mouth. Adi and Yongcheow were frozen in apprehension. Even the crew, flocked on the sand between the tents, had turned to stare.

Mokoya's diaphragm squeezed, as though the heaviness infesting her belly was pulling the drawstrings tight. She kept her jaw clamped shut as her throat spasmed.

"Okay," Adi abruptly said into the quiet. "We do it."

Yongcheow shot her a look of betrayal, his mouth forming a protest. Adi stopped him with a glance. Mokoya watched the split-second exchange and realized that they had talked while she was away. Filaments of worry wormed through her chest. What had they discussed? What had they agreed on?

"We go at next sunrise," Adi said. "And we only have a few hours to prepare. So come. Chop-chop."

~

On the periphery of the camp, Mokoya found a series of cracked shale outcrops the right size and shape for cudgel practice. Dozens of yields away, Adi's crew sat under the gentle circles of sunball-light, sharing spiced tea and tall tales before the hunt. Strains of their laughter drifted over, as though mocking her. The ink of the sky diluted in anticipation of the coming sunrise. Mokoya had ten minutes left to get ready.

She inhaled, becoming hyperaware of her body in relation to the rest of the world: her feet light on the ground, the cudgel loose in her hand, the heaviness solid in her stomach.

She exhaled, and in that breath, the world slowed around her.

Mokoya struck. She was lightning, she was quicksilver, she was the sun that flew across the sky. Her cudgel struck the rock six times in succession, each blow landing with a crack. Needle-precise fractures shot across the rock in dark lines.

She pulled skeins of metal-nature together. The cudgel came to life, its core singing with electricity. Mokoya spun in the sand. The bolt arced and struck the rock, dead center.

It shattered. Shale fragments plowed into the sand, and dust billowed up in circles.

Mokoya moved on to the next outcrop.

She was most alive like this, conscious thought sub-sumed beneath layers of movement. Focused on destruc-tion, she didn't have to think about other things. Like seeing Thennjay again, after two years on the run, or the depth of betrayal she felt at Akeha for summoning him here.

Part of her wanted to die in glorious battle against the naga, just because she knew it would hurt Akeha. It'd serve him right, thinking that he knew what to do better than she did. Turtle bastard.

The Slack unmake them all. She swore as she struck the columns of rock over and over. *Fuck. Shit. Kanin—nahbeh—chao—cheebye—*

*You've learned to swear like a southern merchant,* her brother had said, back in the city. He'd sounded proud of the fact.

Mokoya slammed one end of the cudgel into the sand so hard it stayed upright. Her heart galloped in her chest, and she didn't know how much of it was exertion, and how much of it was nerves. She wanted to explode the same way the columns of rock had.

She let her cheeks billow with breath several times. Misery and anger blossomed in bright colors over her right arm. No good. Mokoya tightened her cloak over her shoulders, as if that would hide it.

Phoenix had been watching her from a safe distance.

Mokoya went over and plunged a hand into her saddle-bag, desperately seeking a capture pearl. Just one memory, any memory. A lottery of the past.

She extracted her hand from the bag. In her trembling fingers, a sunrise-pink capture pearl shimmered. Yes. This would do. Mokoya settled cross-legged against Phoenix and tempered her breathing. As she gently tensed through the pearl's contents, the vision unfolded in her head, brilliant and crisp as the day it was made.

Eien, round-cheeked and sticky, pointed to belts and buttons with their blunt fingers, saying "Yim? Yim?"

A bright afternoon eight years ago. Eien, new to talking, too young to have thought about gender, testing out their favorite word "khim," which their tender tongue could not yet shape. *Yim.* Every reflective surface got pointed to and interrogated: "Yim? Yim?"

A belly laugh, and there was Thennjay, sitting across from them in the traveling cart. Broad-shouldered, shaven-headed, dimpled as she remembered him. Ceremonial saffron vivid against the deep rosewood tones of his skin. Eien detached from her lap and bounced toward him. Their father lifted them into his arms, planting a kiss on their head, his smile ivory-brilliant. The child reached for the bangles on his arm. "Yim!"

"Oei."

Mokoya opened her eyes very slowly, lingering in the

golden light for another half second. In the grayish predawn, she found Adi standing over her, arms akimbo, genial expression displaced by a frown. A sunball glowed and bobbed beside her.

"You're really moody today, you know?"

"I'm fine." Mokoya cracked her neck, her shoulders.

"Sure or not?" Adi's tone made clear which side of the divide her opinions fell upon.

Mokoya pulled her cloak over her arm. "You don't have to worry. I won't jeopardize the hunt."

"You think I'm worried about the hunt?"

Mokoya had come Adi's way two years ago, a strange and angry woman with a giant raptor and a bagful of unfixable problems. Adi had looked that mess and somehow still said, *Come with us.*

Mokoya sighed. "You don't have to worry about me."

"Okay. Can." Adi shook her head wryly. She wasn't fond of arguing, either. "Come. It's time already."

# Chapter Three

**THE RISING SUN BREATHED** the sky to life. It sloughed through a gamut of clammy blues before warming to pink, its skin scarred with strips of cloud. Astride Phoenix, Mokoya smelled water on the air, a metallic tang cleaner than blood and not quite as sharp.

The caverns chosen by the naga had a single mouth, a wide slash in the rock that could swallow Phoenix twenty times over. A hundred yields to its left lay the scrub-ringed clearing where the crew waited with hungry nets.

Mokoya was the bait.

She sent her soundball, a softly glowing, plum-sized sphere laden with the cries of naga prey, floating toward the cave mouth. Tensing through metal-nature woke the device and triggered a piercing blast: the trumpeting call of a tuapeh. A temptingly juicy meal for a naga.

Silence followed. Stillness. The cave mouth remained undisturbed.

Mokoya counted to six, then tensed again. Another sound.

Phoenix shuffled, nervous.

She couldn't be wrong. The prickle rippling through her lizard arm meant the naga was close by.

A shadow passed across the ground: wings, still distant, still indistinct. Startled, Mokoya looked up. The new sun greeted her, smearing green afterimage into her vision. She squinted.

High overhead the naga circled, gliding, wings held straight.

Surprise hissed between Mokoya's teeth. The naga had left the cave during the sundown period. But naga had poor night vision. They hunted in daylight.

The beast dipped downward, not vertically as for a landing, but sideways, like a flyby. Still out of their reach, but close enough that Mokoya could pick out the massive tendons in its wings, stretching out from the muscles of the arm, and—

A series of brown strips crisscrossed the naga's pale chest. There was a harness. She had missed it in the panic of her previous encounter.

A harness. That meant—

"There's a rider," Mokoya whispered. A human rider.

The naga beat its wings once. Phoenix braced against the displacement as it sailed to altitude.

It wasn't going to come down. A human rider would know a trap when they saw one.

Mokoya blew air between her lips, and allowed herself one small, soft "cheebye."

Then she tapped her wrist, where a brand-new and un-flattened voice transmitter bravely waited. "Adi. There's a problem."

"Wah lao. What now?"

"I have to bring it down."

"What? Mokoya—"

"Stand by." She shut the transmitter off.

The naga was still circling overhead. Mokoya kicked twice into Phoenix's side in warning. Then she raised her right hand over her head and tensed.

Earth-nature responded. Gravity warped in the pull of the Slack. Everything in Mokoya's radius instantly grew tenfold heavier.

Iron-weight, the naga crashed to land. The ground shuddered, and a crown of dust rushed outward at them.

Metal-nature sang through Mokoya's cudgel, and electricity struck the downed naga, paralyzing one wing.

Mokoya released her hold on earth-nature. The dust cloud jumped in height. She punched through it with water-nature, exposing the naga sprawled on the ground, wings spread, bellowing.

Freed from the weight, Phoenix sprinted toward the beast. Behind her was Adi's crew, making the best of the disarray.

On the naga's back, the rider was a thin figure

cocooned in gray. Mokoya had to get to them.

She braced into a crouch as Phoenix ran up to the naga's paralyzed shoulder. It was ten times her size, easy, radiating exhausted heat. Mokoya leapt up—

—the Slack punched into her—

—and the world tilted. The Grand Monastery. The raptor pens. This dread architecture, with all the bronze gates still intact. The chirrups of young raptors waiting to be fed. Eien's laughter, the way her robes bounced as she skipped forward holding the bucket. The loud clicking from the heater in the center, which Mokoya knew now was the warning sign that one of its pipes, corroded by acid, was about to give way.

She wanted to scream as Eien darted away from her, tracing the path history had already mapped out for her;

the path where Mokoya watched her baby girl run toward the raptors, past the clicking heater, oblivious;

the path where Mokoya smiled indulgently, instead of scooping her up and dragging her to safety, condensing a lead-thick wall of air between them and the heater that was about to—

—vaporize in a ball of angry orange, engulfing her daughter a microsecond before the hot air and gases seared into Mokoya, screaming agony dissolving flesh and bone—

Something jerked Mokoya forward so hard her shoulders popped. Her feet found purchase, planting into something warm and shifting and hard, like muscle, like skin.

She stared into a face. Human. Swathed in gray, long-boned and milk-white. Dark eyes with an intensity that stopped the heart.

The rider. The naga's rider had caught her.

Beneath them the naga bellowed, a wall-shaking sound that traveled up its rib cage. Then it reared. Mokoya's feet slipped. The naga's back rippled as it beat its wings. Air whipped fiercely up, hurricane strength: the paralysis was gone.

The familiar cyclical whine of lightcraft cascaded over the chaos, accompanied by the rhythmic syllables of battle chants. Mokoya knew that sound. She had learned it as a child; she had sung it as an adult. Thennjay. The pugilists had arrived early.

The rider's arms shook, narrow fingers latched to Mokoya's wrists, biting into bone. Even in the chaos, Mokoya could hear the air whistling through their lungs. Those eyes had the pull of a sun. Acting on instinct, Mokoya squeezed hers shut and tensed magnitude back into gravity, forcing the naga toward the ground.

A strange sensation enveloped her, as though a dozen fingers were tracing patterns across her soul. Mokoya swallowed air, and her eyes snapped open. The rider—a woman?—was still staring at her.

Their pale lips moved. "Forgive me." *Forgive me.* A sound heard in the heart, not in the mind. The language sounded archaic and she didn't know why.

Then, like a fishhook through the chest, her connection to the Slack was torn from her. Not destroyed, but pulled out of reach. Mokoya gasped as she detached from the world.

Great power accumulated and released. Something massive moved, like a city falling off a cliff.

"Mokoya. Mokoya!"

She was flat on her back, head throbbing, throat and tongue cottony. Sunlight poured into her eyes. Her wrists felt like they were broken.

Adi leaned farther into her field of vision. "You better not be dead. How am I supposed to explain to your brother?"

Mokoya found the shape of her mouth. "What . . ."

"You asking me?"

Mokoya sat up, and her hips groaned. Everything lay flattened in a twenty-yield radius around her. Adi's crew was in disarray, fighting with the upset raptors. And there, with the grace of drifting petals, were the pugilists descending on the lotus-shaped plates that were the Grand Monastery's signature lightcraft.

The naga, and its rider, were gone. Strangeness upon strangeness. Only now, in the post-adrenaline pulse of the aftermath, did Mokoya realize that they'd used the old genderless pronoun for adults, from before the language changed. A radical? That unplaceable accent.

"There was a rider," Mokoya said. "Did you see?"

"Yah, I'm not blind. Who was it? A Tensor?"

"Maybe. I don't know." She'd never seen slackcraft done that way. And Tensors were so strict about the proper methods. "They took my slackcrafting ability and used it to—" Words failed her. "I don't know what they did."

"The whole naga disappeared. Just like that." Adi snapped her fingers. "Crazy."

The last of the pugilists, his robes oxblood and saffron, disembarked from his lightcraft. As he dropped to the ground he called out, "Hoy!"

Phoenix sprang to meet the tall figure in delight, her feet kicking up compacted sand. "Hey, girl, hey," Thennjay said, staggering under the assault of her massive snout. "How are you, girl? Hey, hey."

Thennjay Satyaparathnam liked to say he had achieved two distinctions in life: becoming youngest Head Abbot in the history of the Grand Monastery, and also its tallest. Mokoya liked to add that he was also the Head Abbot who had discarded the greatest number of monastic vows—most notably that of chastity—so perhaps there should be a third distinction.

The son of a fire breather and a stilt walker, Thennjay had once thought he would spend his life in a circus, doing magic tricks and juggling things for money. Then Mokoya received her vision. The fortunes had intervened. He became the Gauri street mutt turned Head Abbot. At their wedding, he had made the predictable "I was the man of her dreams" joke, and Mokoya had almost managed not to punch him. She had made him pay for it that night.

Mokoya found her feet and folded her arms as he approached. "Well, look who I found," he said.

"What are you doing out here, Thenn?"

"You know," he said, looking out at the ruined landscape. "Just seeing the sights."

She didn't unfold her arms. He sighed. "Akeha told me where to find you. Seemed like you needed help."

"When I need help, I ask."

"Do you?"

Mokoya's lips tightened.

Adi nodded at Thennjay. They corresponded sometimes, a fact that Mokoya did her best to ignore. "Ey, Mister Head Abbot," her captain said brightly, "how's life in the Grand Monastery?"

He laughed. "It's been better. Like those days before my beloved ran off to hunt naga in the wilderness."

Adi snorted. Mokoya didn't laugh. Silence descended

around them. Thennjay looked at the floor.

Adi sighed. "Okay. Come, lah, got a lot of work to do." Something in the background caught her attention, a boneheaded nephew: "Oei, Faizal! It's backward, lah! Bodoh." She scuttled off to handle the situation. A graceful exit, all things considered.

Thennjay studied Mokoya's face carefully. "It's good to see you, Nao," he said, gently.

"Good for you," she said. Her chest twinged as she said it, like someone had pulled a string too hard and it had snapped, but she wasn't about to take it back. She ducked down to pick her cudgel off the floor, refusing to look at Thennjay's face. She imagined it must hurt still, after all these years, her brushing him off. She didn't want to know.

# Chapter Four

"I TOLD YOU we shouldn't have gone after it," Yongcheow said. His chin was pointed in Mokoya's direction, bright and bitter triumph shining on his face.

"Come on," Thennjay said. "Now's hardly the time . . ."

They had retreated to camp. Sunfall was imminent, marking the end of the day-cycles. A pot of stew was boiling somewhere among the tents, spicing the air with notes of cardamom and star anise. Good to know someone still had appetite left.

Yongcheow ignored Thennjay. "You didn't want to listen, did you? You never listen."

"Did anyone die?" Mokoya snapped. When nobody responded, she said, "No. Nobody died. And we learned something important." She stared at Yongcheow. "Which we wouldn't have if we'd stayed in our tents."

Adi said, "The two of you are really getting on my nerves."

Thennjay's deep voice rumbled over their exchanges. "Right now the most important thing is to decide what we do next."

"I'm going back to Bataanar," Yongcheow said. "I need to talk to the Machinist leadership. Lady Han must hear of this. I can't speak to her here."

"Oh, good. So there's no need for discussion, then," Mokoya said.

"Nao—"

"I'm not going back," Mokoya said. "That naga is still loose in the desert. We need to find out where it's gone."

"Yah," Adi said. "Sooner or later it'll come back. We need to be prepared."

"It doesn't have to be one or the other," Thennjay said. "We can split up. Half the pugilists can follow Yongcheow to Bataanar, just in case. The other half can stay here—with you—and try to track that creature down." He hesitated. "I'll stay with you."

Mokoya fastened her arms across her chest. "We don't need your help."

"Hello," Adi said. "You don't put words in my mouth, okay? *I* want him to stay. You think you one person enough to stop that thing?"

"Fine," Mokoya said. "Do whatever. I don't care." It was Adi's crew. She was tired and her hip hurt and her chest hurt, and people could do whatever they wanted; it didn't concern her. She turned and walked away.

～

The edge of the Copper Oasis lay a hundred yields from the camp, its borders tender and marshy, its waters glossy black and unfathomable in the moonlight. Mokoya stood in front of that broad mirror, vast enough to vanish into the horizon, and wondered what it would be like to walk into its cool embrace, to let the oasis close its gentle hands over her head. She imagined silence, darkness, eternal bliss. Her lungs finally full and content.

She snapped herself out of her reverie. There was still plenty of work to do.

The vision of Eien's death lay curled like a fist on her belt, an explosive housed in thin glass walls. She thought about hurling it into the dark as hard as she could, gifting the oasis its oil-slick contents. But she didn't have that many capture pearls to waste. Gingerly she removed it from the capture box and undid the knots in the Slack. Light dissipated as the memory was cast back into nothingness, where it belonged.

She wanted to vomit.

Behind her, oasis grass rustled. Mokoya knew who it was before she spoke: Adi, come to make sure Mokoya was all right, as if she didn't have enough to worry about herself.

"I'm fine," Mokoya said preemptively. And then, sensing that this was too much of a lie even for her, amended it to "I'll be fine."

Adi stood next to her and sighed. "Mokoya, I'm sorry."

"What are you apologizing for?"

"The death anniversary is tomorrow, right? I forgot. That's why you're so moody."

"It's . . ." Adi wasn't wrong. "It's nothing, compared with everything else going on. I should be the one apologizing." She shook her head. "I know Yongcheow's just trying to help."

"And your husband also."

"And him too."

They looked out over the waters in silence.

"I'm sorry," Mokoya said. "I know I shouldn't be like this. It's been four years. I should be better. But . . ." She pushed at blades of oasis grass with her toes. "It hasn't gotten better. I thought it would get better."

"It won't get better just because you want it."

Mokoya listened to the soft sound of water fidgeting against the land.

Adi looked at the moon. "You know, my son died ten years ago. So long ago. All the other small ones, grown big already. But I still get sad on his birthday." As Mokoya managed her breathing, the smallest chuckle escaped her friend. "Birth day, death day. Same day."

There was a crack in Adi's voice, the barest hint of a wobble. That was enough for Mokoya to come undone. Adi stood by while she struggled through the wave of emotions that swept her, not saying anything, just being there.

When she could speak again she said, "I'm sorry, Adi. And . . . thank you."

Another rustle in the grass. This time, it was Yongcheow, and from his expression, she knew that he'd been sent by Thennjay, to fuss over her like an injured child. He froze when he caught sight of Mokoya's face.

"You don't have to apologize," she said, before he could start.

He had stopped several yields away from her. "I . . . must. I've acted uncharitably toward you."

"I tend to bring that out in people."

"Mokoya, I . . . I regret my behavior. I should have been gentler."

"There's no need to apologize."

Yongcheow looked like he was about to say something more. Instead, he glanced away, wetting his cracked lips.

Mokoya said, "And you, do you return to Bataanar now?"

"Yes."

She nodded. "Send Akeha my regards. Tell him . . ." She tried to think of something smart and pithy to say. "Tell him not to blow anything up."

Yongcheow sighed. "Please, stay safe. I don't know how I would deal with him if something happens to you."

~

Mokoya found Thennjay playing a game with Phoenix just beyond the boundary of the tents. Fist-sized chunks of jerky lay in his lap, hammocked in the folds of his robes. "Ready, girl?"

Phoenix's tail feathers rustled. He hefted a chunk, testing its weight. "Okay, get it!"

*Thwack.* "That's a good girl. Come on, get this one."

Mokoya leaned against the side of Thennjay's tent and watched the trajectories of several more treats. Thennjay's laugh had the same deep growl it did when he used to play with Eien.

She thought, *I miss this. I miss happiness.* It sounded even sadder when put into words.

"I know I have shapely shoulders," Thennjay finally said, without turning around, "but you could come talk to my face. It's just as attractive, you know."

Mokoya huffed, but came toward him anyway. She had brought a peace offering wrapped in cloth: a warm clay pot, fragrant with shallot oil. "Dinner," she said. "Peanut congee."

He lifted the lid and sniffed. "I was hoping for some meat bone tea. Akeha says Yongcheow's *has* to be tried."

In the kitchen, Yongcheow had once managed to set a pan of water on fire. "Oh. You're making a joke."

He smiled at her. She let him.

As he tucked into the congee, Mokoya carefully sat next to him, hooking her arms around her knees. Phoenix rolled onto the sand in front of them and let out a slow, satisfied breath of air.

"She knows who you are," Mokoya said, pointedly.

Around a mouthful of food, Thennjay countered, "She remembers that I helped raise her for several years. Any raptor from the monastery would do the same." He swallowed. "It doesn't mean she's special, Nao."

This was an old argument between them, perhaps too old. Mokoya had left the Grand Monastery after she grew sick of hearing every iteration, every branch of the conversation. She didn't know why she was still arguing it.

Phoenix snuffled, and sand blew up in a cloud. Mokoya listened to the soft song of the desert winds, much calmer than they had been a sun-cycle ago.

Eventually, she said, "Why are you here, Thennjay?"

"Do you really have to ask?"

She shrugged. Yes, no. Who knew?

Thennjay put the clay pot down. Gentle fingers parted the fringe of hair skirting the bones of her neck, as though he were studying the scars that blossomed from her shoulder. "I wanted to see you."

Mokoya pushed her toes deeper into the sand. He said, "I spent two anniversaries alone. It was miserable.

And I knew asking you to come back wouldn't work, so . . ." He shrugged and slapped his thighs. "The eagle moves where the mountain cannot."

"So this was your idea? Not Akeha's?"

"Well. If you need to, you can split the blame between us." A half smile emerged on his expression. "Admit it—it helps having us around."

She studied his profile in the milky sunball light. "It's a long way to travel from Chengbee. You could have just called."

"I wanted to see you," he repeated.

She let that hang in the air between them. A significant part of her, centered in her chest, wanted to let her knees fall and rest against his. Wanted to settle her body weight against his and go to sleep, as though they lived in brighter and easier times.

"I worry about you," he said.

"You don't have to."

He cautiously put his arm around her shoulders. She allowed him the action, but didn't lean into his touch. His hand was warm through the cloak she had pulled tight around her shoulders, a blanket over lizardflesh that concealed the colors bleeding across the skin.

"Four years have gone by," he said, putting words down like a man walking across a rotting bridge. "You have to stop running at some point. You have to return."

"To stop running doesn't mean to return."

"I don't mean to me, or to the Grand Monastery, or even to Chengbee. I meant to life, Nao. You have to come back. I see you, I hear about what you're doing, and I know you're walking around with this sheet of glass between you and the world. You have to break it sometime."

She didn't want to turn this into an argument. She was tired. It was the fourth anniversary, and he had traveled all the way here to see her. He didn't deserve it.

Great Slack, but she was tired.

He lifted her chin and studied the shadows of her countenance. "Once upon a time, I met someone bold and bright as a leaping river. A silver thread in the Slack, shining against all the reds and the blues. Now I don't know where she's gone."

*She died,* Mokoya thought. *She died in the explosion that took her daughter's life.*

Thennjay grew quiet. "I'm sorry. I won't push you, Nao. That rarely ends well."

She felt sorry for him. "Thenn, I'm glad you're here." And she meant it, too. "I truly am."

He hugged her shoulders and kissed the top of her head. A measured, cautious response. "I'm glad to see you too." When he got up and went into his tent, she didn't follow.

# Chapter Five

**MOKOYA COULD NOT SLEEP.** She lay on the coarse fabric of her bedroll, the skin of her neck itching, strange prickles running up and down the lizard arm. The opening of the First Sutra rolled over and over in her head—*the Slack is all, and all is the Slack*—and it formed a barrier between her and sleep. Yet she knew if she stopped, if she gave her mind space to expand like a black sponge, she would see things she did not want to see.

She sat up, shivering. Her capture pearls were arrayed in a glowing line by the bed, colors like lanterns on the Double-Seventh Night. Mokoya knew their contents by sight. If she wanted, she could lose herself in fragments of better times: The riotous joy of Eien's fifth birthday celebration. Games of eagle-and-chicken with Akeha as a child. Her wedding night, if she wanted to exhaust herself into slumber. She just had to reach out.

Her fingers trembled, and she pulled away.

Mokoya left the tent, stepping into the salmon-tinted sunrise. The second night-cycle was beginning: she'd lost three hours of sleep she wasn't going to get anyway. The changing air spread a chill through her from the lungs outward. A variety of options lay open to her. She could go to Thennjay's tent to wake him. She could practice sparring. She could run around the oasis, feet sinking into the unstable sands.

But Mokoya looked in the direction of the canyons and wondered what the naga and its human handler were doing with the new sunrise. Would they follow the patterns imposed by human society and continue to rest? Or would the naga bow to its instincts and hunt again?

Who were they, and what did they want?

Mokoya took several slow steps forward. There was stupidly reckless behavior, and then there was behavior so reckless it bordered on the suicidal. But she had decided. It was better than staying here and doing nothing. Nothing except driving herself into greater madness.

~

The cave mouth stood unchanged in the new sunlight. Mokoya stopped Phoenix a dozen yields from the rock face and dismounted with a frown.

A barrier shimmered in the air across the length of the rock, a light fuzz that became apparent only from certain angles. When Mokoya pressed her fingers into its boundary, the air sparked and threads of slackcraft tightened around her hand. She pulled back before it could draw blood.

In her mindeye the barrier stood as an intricate tapestry, fine ropes from each of the five natures braided into astounding, geometric patterns. Tessellations built upon tessellations in a palimpsest of slackcraft. Unpicking it would take time and skill—if it was even possible. Mokoya didn't know where to start.

So she started with brute force.

She tore into the center of the pattern, where a rosette of connections spread out into a five-pointed star. She hoped to sever the threads of Slack-connections, or simply pull them loose.

In the physical world, the barrier writhed and crackled. A riot of colors flashed in the air, perfuming it with the tang of burning metal.

The barrier held. The interlocked threads showed no sign of weakness. When Mokoya released her grip in exhaustion, they sprang back whole and unaffected.

Then the Slack puckered, and the woven threads sublimed into nothing. They did not break or unravel: they simply vanished, like ice held over a flame. The barrier slid out of existence, freeing the air on either side of it.

A small pop, a strange deformation in the Slack, and a gray-clad figure stood in front of her.

"Tensor Sanao Mokoya," they said, their eyes wide and unblinking.

Mokoya's cudgel sprang to life. "You." She struck, sending a bolt in their direction.

A green hexagon flashed in front of the stranger. "Wait," they gasped.

The hexagon hadn't deflected the bolt: it had absorbed the energy instead. Its pattern in the Slack had the same complexity as the bigger barrier, appearing and vanishing in an instant. Mokoya had never seen anyone call up slackcraft that intricate so quickly. The cudgel stayed ready in her hand. "Who are you?"

"I am called Rider," they said. Mokoya hadn't heard wrong, then: they used the archaic, gender-neutral "I" that had died out centuries ago.

"I don't want your name. Who sent you?"

"No one sent me. I am here of my own accord."

"You're lying."

They stepped back in fear and stumbled as the sandy ground turned traitor. They had long, thin limbs like a Quarterlander and seemed unsteady on their feet. "Please," they said, "I have no quarrel with you, Tensor Sanao—"

"Did the Protectorate send you?"

Fear overwhelmed their expression. A pop, a deformation in the Slack: they were gone.

"Cheebye!" Mokoya ran forward to the space formerly occupied by Rider. Her lip curled. Perking up, Phoenix fell in behind her, excited for another hunt. "Stay," Mokoya snapped. "Stay out here. And *wait.*"

She sprinted into the cave mouth, which drilled through rock in a broad tunnel. Ahead was the promise of light, and running water. The passageway echoed with the sound of an angry naga, and wind gusted over her in waves, increasing in frequency. Wing beats.

Mokoya ran faster.

She burst into the cavern before the naga could take flight. This hollow in the sandstone was huge, a hundred yields wide and half as high. Sunlight punched through on the left where water cascaded in a shimmering curtain, fringed by brilliant splotches of colors: bloodreeds, orange lilies, clumps of cattails.

On the right was the naga, wings spread to the roof of the cavern, bellowing as Rider tried to coax it into flight. Mokoya tensed through earth-nature, the same trick she'd employed earlier, pulling the beast down with gravity. It folded with a groan, joints collapsing under pressure.

"Please stop," Rider begged. "Don't hurt her—she has done nothing."

Mokoya blinked, releasing her hold on earth-nature. The stranger's plea held a note of something she hadn't expected: protectiveness. Vulnerability and fear, too—the entreaty of someone afraid of losing something precious. She kept her grip firm on her cudgel, but she let them dismount, dropping to the soft sand of the cavern.

The naga hissed and backed away, putting more space between itself and Mokoya. Rider sang, a keening note, as they slid soothing hands over the creature's neck and bearded head. The naga calmed, but its luminous eyes—pupils slitted through mint-green—remained fixed on Mokoya.

"Bramble remembers you from before," Rider said. "It's not a good memory. You traumatized her."

"You're not Protectorate," Mokoya said.

"No."

Things were falling into place. The odd style of slackcraft, the unusual physique, the heavy accent: Rider was a Quarterlander. Of course they had a naga. Of course they rode on it. They belonged to people who crossed the Demons' Ocean in ships of shell and bone that sluiced beneath the untamable waves. Riding such a beast would be easy as crossing a bridge, unremarkable as eating rice. And of course they couldn't be a Tensor. There'd never been a Quarterlander admitted into the Tensorate Academy. That would cause such a stir that even washerfolk in Katau Kebang would be gossiping about it.

Mokoya let her shoulders drop, but she continued to

hold her cudgel like a weapon. "What are you doing here?"

Rider was about to answer when the naga growled. Behind them, Phoenix had edged into the cavern, feathers alert and erect, mouth open to show teeth.

"I told you to stay outside," Mokoya scolded.

Phoenix hooted mournfully.

"Is this her?" Rider asked. When Mokoya frowned they clarified: "Your daughter."

Mokoya exhaled very slowly, her organs curdling into tallow.

Rider said, to her silence, "There are rumors of the accident that killed your daughter. They say that when she died, you grafted her pattern in the Slack onto a young raptor. Is this her? She's very large. And the pattern she makes is interesting."

Their tone was untainted by judgment or condescension. If anything, they sounded curious.

She swallowed. And then she said, "Yes."

The memory shivered through her: the smell of blood, burnt flesh, oily smoke; an impression of pain that was happening to some other body in some other world; the Slack shining wide and lucid around her; the glow of knots and threads that was Eien beginning to disintegrate; the movement she made pulling it to the nearest incandescence, tying it in place, tying it firm, so it wouldn't be lost—

*Focus. Focus. Look at the falling water. Look at the light refracted, dancing over the ground. Breathe.*

A delicate expression—not quite a smile, not quite a look of curiosity—had come over Rider. They appeared to have forgotten Mokoya was there. One pop through the Slack, and they appeared before Phoenix, who reared back in terror.

"Hush," Mokoya said, hurrying forward, but Rider remained perfectly still, their palms held out to Phoenix. The raptor hesitated, then lowered her snout and sniffed their hands, then their arms, their face, their neck.

Rider's face lit up with wonder. "She is lovely." They stroked the soft, pebbled skin of her nose, the boundary where flesh ceded to feather.

Mokoya started to breathe normally again. When Rider turned once more to look at her, she said, "Who are you? What are you doing here?"

"A question that cannot be answered simply. Come sit by me, Sanao Mokoya. We should talk."

They smiled at her, and there was something oddly alluring in that. Something transient and precious, like the sun glowing across paving stones during the minute that it fell. Damned if Mokoya could put it into words that made more sense. Against her better judgment, she nodded.

~

"I was born in Katau Kebang, in Banturong, on the border of the Demons' Ocean. My parents were merchants. But the doctors diagnosed an illness, a disease of the bones and joints. So my parents sold me to Quarterlanders, in hopes that my path to adulthood would be easier in the half gravity."

The two of them sat cross-legged in the cavern, knee-to-knee, close enough that Mokoya could follow the easy rise and fall of Rider's chest. They had a soft oval face of Kuanjin extraction, and the skin on their hands was translucent enough Mokoya could count the veins. But despite how sallow their face was, their eyes burned with a passion and intensity that snared the attention and refused to let it go.

"When I was twenty," Rider said, "I took Bramble across the Demons' Ocean. I wanted to find my family, the ones who had given me away. But I was told they had relocated from Banturong, and moved back to the capital city. So it was to the capital city that I traveled. Do you follow, Tensor Sanao?"

"Just call me Mokoya. Please."

"Mokoya." Rider sounded it in their mouth, as though testing out its fit. They smiled like it pleased them. "Mokoya."

"So," Mokoya said, "you went to Chengbee."

"Yes. And in the capital I met a woman. Tan Khimyan."

She frowned. "I know that name."

"You should. She moved to Bataanar recently, as an advisor to Raja Choonghey. It was at his invitation. Mokoya."

Yes—Akeha had mentioned her—that was why the name was familiar. "They're friends?"

"Perhaps too shallow a description for their relationship, Mokoya. The two became close around Raja Ponchak's death. When she was very ill, Ponchak went to the capital to seek treatment. That is how Khimyan and Choonghey met."

A suspicious coincidence—or perhaps not a coincidence. She remembered Akeha referring to Tan Khimyan as an adversary. *The* adversary, even.

"Keep talking."

As they had been speaking, Phoenix had started making curious overtures to the other beast in the cavern: creeping up, bumping her snout against Bramble's shoulder, then scuttling away. The naga rumbled, equally curious and equally cautious.

Rider said, "It is necessary you know this, Mokoya. Khimyan and I were intimately involved. An arrangement that, in hindsight, was ill-advised on my part. But it allowed me to become privy to some of the things she did in secret."

Mokoya raised an eyebrow, and Rider laughed, a sound like chimes on the wind. "Not of the sort you are imagining, Mokoya."

"I'm sorry. Please continue." She liked the way her name sounded in their mouth, the vowels round and gentle. She kept her hands pressed to her thighs, lest they betray her.

"Khimyan kept company with a group of Tensors who were conducting experiments on a clutch of captive young naga. They were inspired by what you achieved with Phoenix. They wanted to replicate it, surpass it even."

A shiver passed through Mokoya, starting from the deep of her chest and spreading to her fingers and toes. "I'm glad my personal tragedy was so inspirational," she said through her teeth.

Rider's lips curved. Vindictiveness looked foreign on the soft lines of their face, yet the expression was also corrosively genuine. "I reported them to the Tensorate. It was the first thing I did when I escaped."

"Escaped?"

They hesitated. "Khimyan ... has ways of trapping people by her side. I left when she brought home another girl, another child who was unwell and would be entirely reliant upon her. I had realized that she would never change. She saw those around her as curiosities, not people." They shifted their weight slightly, bumping their knees against Mokoya's. "And I feared she might take Bramble for experiments. Mokoya."

"That sounds like a terrible thing to be put through. My sympathies."

They shrugged, a fluid motion of the shoulders. "Because of what I did, Khimyan was expelled from the Tensorate and had to leave the city. So there was some justice, after all."

"So they were successful, these Tensors? With their experiment?"

Rider nodded.

Mokoya's mind chugged through this information, trawling for the dregs of logic that had to be contained within. So the rumors the Machinists heard had been right. But again, not *wholly*. If this was the work of bored, arrogant Tensors, and not instructions from the Protector—

Phoenix barked: a child sound, short and high. When Mokoya looked, she was darting away from a swipe of Bramble's clawed wings, head bobbing playfully. The naga grumbled, and its tail flicked, scales and spikes iridescent in the dimness.

"You still haven't answered my question," Mokoya said.

"Which one, Mokoya?"

"What are you doing here?"

"Have I not given you enough clues to answer it yourself?"

"I want to hear you say it."

Rider folded their hands in the loose gray of their lap, the shape of their wrist bones pulling at Mokoya's attention. "You and I seek the same thing, Mokoya. The naga that these Tensors created. It has come to Bataanar and nests nearby, somewhere in the desert."

Mokoya looked briefly at Bramble, then back at Rider. "There is a second naga?"

"Yes."

"Who summons it?"

Rider tilted their head, frowning. Mokoya got more direct: "Is this part of a Protectorate plan to destroy Bataanar?"

"Ah." Understanding brightened Rider's expression. "You are a Machinist. Of course—that would be your primary interest. Yes." Their gaze briefly flicked toward the light puncturing the cavern. "This is no Protectorate plot, Mokoya. Whatever the naga's purpose here, it has nothing to do with crushing the Machinist movement."

Rider spoke with a conviction that would have been suspicious, if what they were saying didn't make so much *sense.* In Mokoya's head, the abnormalities of this saga were rearranging themselves into a new shape, like a tangram. A vast, unwieldy political conspiracy folded into a petty, personal drama: not a plot to destroy a city, but the journey of an abandoned creature seeking its creator. "Is the city in danger?"

"I do not suspect so, Mokoya. There is little benefit to be gained from harming it."

A capsule of relief burst over Mokoya, and she relaxed into its cooling embrace. Out of everything, she could at least set aside her worry about the immediate fate of Bataanar, that citadel of stone and white clay protecting her brother.

"Come back with me to camp," she said. "You need to meet my crew leader." *And my husband.* "We have a lot to discuss."

"Do the rest of your crew also not sleep?"

Mokoya chuckled: she had forgotten the time. "Come tomorrow morning, then, at first sunrise."

"Or you could remain with me for the rest of the night."

Mokoya blinked. Rider leaned forward, and the closeness of their body, the heat of it mingling with her own, told her she hadn't misunderstood their meaning. "I find you attractive," Rider said, "and from your responses, I think you feel the attraction mutual. Why not lie with me?"

She laughed. This wasn't the first time she'd been so

barefacedly propositioned, naturally. But she hadn't expected this treatment out here, far from the fast-and-loose environs of red-lantern wine houses. And Rider had guessed right: Mokoya had been poorer at obscuring her base desires than she thought.

Inexplicably, she shook her head. Among Adi's crew she had gained a reputation for spending each night in a city in a different bed. And Thennjay had always urged her to take on more lovers, not fewer. She couldn't articulate why she was refusing something so freely given.

Rider sat back, reestablishing space between them. They seemed calm. "I apologize if I was too forward."

"You weren't. I just—" She shivered, trying to put aside thoughts of Rider's cool skin next to hers. "You saw my vision, didn't you?"

"I did, Mokoya."

"And you still want to get in bed with that?"

Confusion worked through Rider's face. Mokoya sighed and said, "Now's not a good time." She had no better explanation.

"I understand. Wait here, then." Again, that pop in the air, that sideways shift through the Slack. Rider transported across the cavern, their lithe form kneeling to search through the bags tied to Bramble's harness. Mokoya had begun to understand that the intricate patterns of their slackcraft were not manually created, but generated from the processes that underlay the mysterious Quarterlandish style of tensing.

Rider returned to her in a half crouch, one hand steadying themselves on Mokoya's lap. With the other, they pressed a small, warm object into Mokoya's hand.

It was a bronze dodecahedron, hollow in the center, each of its twelve faces taking the form of a zodiac animal. Mokoya turned it round, marveling at the artistry in the stylized figures, the bright eyes, the pointed teeth.

"It's an anchor," Rider said.

"What does that mean? What does it anchor?"

"I fold the Slack to travel, as you must have noticed." Now Mokoya had a name for the process. "However, my control of the method is effective only at short distances. To travel to distant places, I must have an anchor in the place I wish to go. It ensures I do not materialize inside a wall, or outside a third-floor window."

Touching the anchor's shape in the Slack stirred up dormant memories in the slow pulp of Mokoya's mind. Honeylemon summer days, tender fruit slices dipped in sugar and chili. Some sort of spell woven into the body of the anchor, almost like a signature. Gooseflesh and pleasure played across her arms, a blush of warmth spreading red.

A small smile tugged at Rider's lips. "Are you certain you do not wish to stay?"

Mokoya sighed and tucked the anchor into a waist pouch. She would not give in to temptation.

Rider understood. "We will meet again soon, Mokoya."

~

Mokoya managed to get halfway to camp before she changed her mind and turned around. She gave herself that much credit, at least.

Rider was curled up on their sleeping mat, loosely swathed in a gossamer layer of muslin, when she returned. They sat up, blinking heavy lids. "Mokoya?"

Mokoya stood silently by the bed, drinking in the long limbs with their slight musculature, the shape of their hips and breasts, the feast of strange characters that spread across their yoghurt complexion.

Still saying nothing, she unfastened the collar of her cloak and pointedly, deliberately, began to undress.

"Mokoya." Rider watched intensely, a smile spreading along their lips, pomegranate-ripe and slow as salt. Wrapped in the gravity of their attention, Mokoya adjusted her movements into a calibrated dance.

Rider reached up and pulled her into a closer orbit. "Mokoya," they whispered, as her lips descended upon their neck. "Mokoya," they repeated, as those lips continued their pilgrimage downward. Rider's voice swelled with breath as Mokoya journeyed over the words on their skin, imagining those radicals spelling commandments, poetry, laws of the universe. *Mokoya. Mokoya.* The world outside faded away. Mokoya closed her eyes and let herself sink into bliss, her mind utterly blank except for those three syllables, tumbling over and over again from Rider's lips.

# Chapter Six

MOKOYA WOKE to the day's first sunrise warming the cavern, casting waterfall light on the far wall. Bramble and Phoenix were quiescent in the corner, a gentle heap of snouts tucked into tails, rib cages rising and falling.

Rider, too, remained in the drifts of sleep, curled against Mokoya's shoulder, loops of hair loose around their face. Peace sat languid and unfamiliar in her chest: not the peace of familiar comforts, of old beddings and well-worn grooves in stone, but a clear kind of peace, like an ocean with stones at the bottom, its surface jade-blue and throwing off sunlight.

Mokoya studied Rider's features, puzzled by the emotions that filled her. She was used to slipping from between the thighs of people for whom names and faces were mere formalities, soon to be forgotten. Yet here she was, imagining futures with this person whose history and mind were gray blanks to her. But what bright futures they were! Days spent hunting, nights spent entwined like this. She was not too old and broken to be snagged on the dangerous barbs of hope.

*You idiot. You chicken-headed idiot.*

Rider stirred as if they could hear her thoughts. *Mokoya*, they mouthed, as if still testing her name on their tongue.

"Did you rest well?" she asked.

"A little too well." In the quiet, Rider traced the pebbled ridges on her right arm, fingers dancing on the border where lizard skin lapped at the brown twists of scar tissue. The arm was a rich crimson now, a wild and prosperous shade Mokoya had rarely displayed since she'd gotten the graft. "The colors change. Do they mean anything?"

"They're controlled by my mood. The doctors took the graft from a blue horned lizard, which uses colors to communicate. Blue is neutral. Green is for sadness, yellow and orange for stress. Black for anger."

"Then what about red?"

"What do you think?"

They smiled.

Mokoya had questions of her own. "Tell me about these markings," she said, tracing a line of them down Rider's arm. Up close, in the light, she recognized the characters as old Kuanjin script, shapes of a dead language known only to obscure scholars. "Why do you have them?"

Rider pressed their face into her chest and mumbled,

"They are a record. They tell the story of my life, the things I want remembered."

"Where did you learn to read them?"

"There are caves in the Quarterlands, deep beneath the skin of the earth, where the walls are covered with thousands upon thousands of these characters. They tell you their names if you ask."

Mokoya shivered, to which Rider said, "I could teach you. The language is not so difficult, especially for a speaker of modern-day Kuanjinwei."

She traced the character strokes printed at the apex of their shoulder. Something stirred under her finger, a phantom flutter of tiny wings. "These aren't ordinary tattoos, are they?"

"No. They are tensed into my skin, into my flesh. I made them so they will burn into my bones upon my death."

"You do these yourself?"

"Of course." They detached from her, rolling onto their back. "I spend many of my days alone, Mokoya. If something happens . . . I do not want my existence to go unremarked upon. I do not want to be an anonymous set of bones scattered in the desert, chanced upon by travelers and discarded."

A springtime of questions flowered in Mokoya's head, and she imagined picking them off one after another, in some version of the future with long, balmy hours for sleep. She imagined comfortable days spent learning new languages, words passing from tongue to tongue.

She stretched. "I have a question."

"What question?"

"When you gave me the anchor yesterday, you said you fold the Slack."

"Yes."

"Can you explain that?" How did one fold something that had no shape, no beginning and no end?

"The Slack knows neither time nor space—it is all that ever was and all that ever will be, connected together. If you bring one point to another, you can travel between them."

"I don't understand." It was like imagining a color invisible to human eyes.

"My time in Chengbee taught me that the way I see the Slack is different from a Tensor's conception of it, Mokoya. Your confusion surprises me, however. Do you not fold the Slack when you seek your visions?"

"No, they come to me unbidden. There's no folding involved, no tensing. It happens when it happens."

"So you have no control over the process?"

"No."

Rider looked at the cavern roof, considering this piece of information. Then they rose to their feet. "Come. I can show you."

They both got dressed and stood in the middle of the cavern.

"Close your eyes," Rider said.

Mokoya cleared her mindeye, and they both became radiant spots against the fabric of the world.

Rider took her hands and tensed.

The world shuddered, sudden and seismic, like the ground was a cloth that had been snatched away. The sound of water washed over her as the air embraced her with cool damp. Droplets flecked her skin. She opened her eyes next to the cascade of oasis water, Rider shimmering before her in the new light.

"Did you feel that?" Rider asked.

"Do it again."

This time, she watched the Slack as it *moved*. Not just the simple motion of tensing, pulling on threads and connections. A wholesale shift. She'd never experienced anything like it.

Rider's voice echoed through the cavern: "Your turn now."

Mokoya blinked. "That's a little—"

"You must try. You have the capability."

Mokoya closed her eyes again. She cleansed her mindeye, recited the First Sutra—

"Forget everything you have learned. It will not help you."

She hissed in annoyance, her focus broken.

Outside the caverns, in the desert, someone shouted her name. Again and again, the sound echoing back and forth. Searching for her. Desperate.

They stared at each other. "Thennjay," Mokoya said. "Something's wrong." She broke into a run, headed for the boundary between cavern and passageway. "Thenn! It's me, I'm in here!"

The whirr of lightcraft tumbled toward her. Whatever momentary peace Mokoya had found was drowned by an acid-sharp flood of adrenaline, thick and frothy in her throat and chest.

Thennjay arrived like an avalanche, presence filling the chamber, gaze sweeping across the scene. "Oh, great."

"What is it?" Mokoya asked. His pinched expression said many things, none of them good.

"Your enjoyable night aside, this day has just taken a massively hell-shat turn—"

"*Thenn.*"

He shut his eyes and forced calmness over his face. "The naga we're hunting? The big one? We found it."

The breath he drew should have warned her what was coming, because it was shaky, and she'd rarely seen him shake. "Nao, it's the size of the sun. And it's attacking Bataanar."

# ACT TWO

# BATAANAR

# Chapter Seven

MOKOYA HAD BEEN DRILLED in basic Slack theory at the Grand Monastery by Master Chong, a tall and hard man, with long steps and a seismic voice that carried across the classroom. Decades later, she could still close her eyes and recall its heavy boom, accompanied by a high chorus of summer crickets.

"The nature of objects is fixed and known. That bucket is red; wood is consumed by fire; ice floats upon water." He strode across the room like he owned it. "Pity the object, for it is trapped in its circumstances. Water can no more freeze in high summer than the sun can decide to stop falling across the sky."

One of the acolytes had snickered. Master Chong had rapped her across the head with his knuckles, cutting her mirth short. His voice had rung out: "Listen carefully, you dogs! Today you learn to break the chains of circumstance. For the masters of the five natures know that the Slack is ever in motion. And through the natures of the Slack, we can change the nature of objects."

*Through the natures of the Slack, we can change the na-*

*ture of objects.* That hot afternoon each acolyte sat, sweat beading, as glasses of water refused to turn into ice, and the walls and floor of the pavilion, warm as a sibling's embrace, mocked their efforts.

Those childhood lessons felt both incalculably distant and intimately close as Phoenix cut full-tilt through the wind, her narrow head lowered, each massive footstep cracking across fresh ice. Mokoya could barely pull the fire from the waters of the oasis fast enough to freeze a pathway beneath them.

If Mokoya had been paying any attention to the math, it would have looked something like this:

Force is mass times acceleration; pressure is force divided by surface area. The load-bearing capacity of ice is a factor of the square of its thickness. A running creature of Phoenix's weight requires a yield of solid ice beneath for support. Volume is length times breadth times height. Two li from the caverns to Bataanar, spanned by a path a yield wide. Ten thousand cubic yields of water to freeze.

But none of that was on her mind. In the window of extreme focus that had opened and swallowed her, all thought was a distraction, a background hum to her actions. Her mindeye superseded her physical senses, the world surrendering to the shimmer of the Slack. Thennjay, mounted on his lightcraft, was a pinprick on the horizon. Behind him, Rider decorated the Slack with polygonal patterns as they pushed Bramble against the wind. Phoenix was falling behind.

Light and pressure exploded hundreds of yields away, as though a volcano had woken into violent enlightenment. *Bataanar.*

Mokoya's eyes snapped open, and fear slammed into her. On the horizon, wavering like a mirage, Bataanar was wreathed in a fiery dome. But it wasn't burning down. The light came from the city's thermal shields, defending it from the creature attacking it.

The naga dwarfed Bramble in size, eclipsing her five to six times over, in a way that rendered math irrelevant. Bloodred clamored against poison-black on its skin. Its spread wings, clawing into the shields, obscured half the city from sight.

The naga screeched, a sound like metal tearing, like gods dying. It pressed its wings into the shields and struck with its hind legs as if it would disembowel the city itself.

How was the naga still alive? How had the shields not burned it to death?

Cracks appeared in the shields, a foul radiance as intense as death. Thermal shields were powerful and complex, setting aflame anything that crossed their threshold. Only Tensors could charge one or hold one against prolonged attack. Bataanar was a working people's city, a blood-and-sweat city, and its reluctant handful of Tensors were better suited to maintaining and charging mining equipment.

Where were the pugilists? Where was her brother? Would they be able to hold it off?

Mokoya's heartbeat made her dizzy. Phoenix could run no faster. She could not fly. They weren't going to make it.

What had Rider said? *The Slack knows neither time nor space. . . . If you bring one point to another, you can travel between them.*

Back in the cavern, she had felt the Slack twist like a child's napkin, sliding away under her.

She returned to the mindeye. The heaving struggle between shield and naga deformed the Slack, tearing a fault line into its fabric. The conflagration looked close enough to touch, but it wasn't. If she could abridge the space between them—

It shouldn't be possible, and yet—

It was like watching a pattern appear out of cloud. The geography of the Slack changed around Mokoya. Everything was still the same, yet the way she saw it had shifted, and if she just pulled it this way—

The Slack folded.

Ice turned to sand under Phoenix. The raptor shrieked as her legs buckled under her, balance lost. Sky and ground lurched. Then came pain: a solid mass of land slamming into Mokoya's head and shoulder and hips. Sand invaded her airways.

Mokoya struggled upright, coughing and spitting. Phoenix was likewise climbing to her feet. The smell of molten metal burned on the air—death smell, industrial-kiln smell. Her clumsy Slack folding had ejected them onto a narrow strip of sand between the oasis and Bataanar. Where the oasis narrowed to a pucker and kissed the side of the city, dozens of boats waited to take workers to the mines. The naga cast a shadow over it all.

The pugilists on their lightcraft were no more than a cloud of mosquitoes, irritating the naga's skin with their tiny lightning bolts. Mokoya saw Adi and the crew huddled limply in the shelter of the oasis inlet.

The naga screamed again. This close to the city, the sound pierced the eardrums like a spear.

Mokoya reached for earth-nature and tensed, hard as she could. Gravity warped, pulling at the naga's massive bulk.

Mokoya felt the naga tense back, and in a moment of shock, she let go. A creature that used slackcraft. Impossible.

Like a cart struck by a falling tree, Bataanar's shields failed.

First principles: water-nature keeps things going in

motion. As the shield exploded, the naga fell forward, bellowing and beating its massive wings to keep afloat. The displaced air knocked Mokoya off her feet. A wing and a hind leg caught watchtowers in their path, shattering the fortifications into loose masonry that pummeled the ground.

Lying on her back, Mokoya watched a single figure, clad in black, leap onto the ruins of the city walls. Akeha. Her twin might disguise himself from others, but she would always know him. He raised a hand, something clutched in it. She felt its pull and knew what it was. "Great Slack, don't—"

Akeha hurled it.

*Cheebye.*

Akeha called them sunballs, but his contraptions were anything but benign givers of light. When her brother made sunballs, he made superweapons. Enclosed in that shell was a minuscule amount of burning gas, invisible to the eye, tensed into so much heat and pressure that the atoms melted, succumbed to one another, and changed their nature. Akeha was working massive amounts of earth-energy, condensed around that single, infinitesimally small point—

Mokoya shielded her face—

He let go.

The explosion hammered through her bones. Something huge fell into the water, a seismic sound, a deep groaning. Acridity flared into her lungs. *Keha, you turtle egg.*

Mokoya's vision cleared in time for Bramble's wings to interrupt the sky. The smaller naga's legs were knives scything into the back of the fallen behemoth as it thrashed in the oasis. The larger naga reared its massive head and slammed into Bramble with one sinuous ripple of the neck. She fell with a desperate, wounded-animal sound.

The grand naga surged into the sky. Tsunami-height waves sent the boats on the inlet crashing into each other, the sound of skeletons being shaken. The beat of its wings flattened sand and shrub in its passage. It headed east. Of course. The segment of desert they hadn't searched yet.

Bramble struggled across the inlet, unable to take to the air. A forlorn figure rested on her back: Rider, slumped in exhaustion. Mokoya's heart contracted painfully as they slid from the harness and crumpled onto the sand.

Mokoya's hip and back reported pain with every stride. Still she ran. Her mind conjured visions of Rider dead, blood emptying onto the hot ground, tattoos flaring red as they burned through their skin.

And then they moved, rising slowly to their feet, taking a step toward her, before folding in two again. In relief, Mokoya closed the distance between them and pulled Rider into her embrace. Their heartbeat stuttered in their neck, in their chest. "Mokoya," they whispered.

"Rest," Mokoya said. "You'll be all right. Thank the fortunes."

"It is as I feared," they said, barely coherent, barely conscious. "This creature . . . what it means. . . ." Their limbs trembled, and they went limp.

"Rider!" Their weight pulled Mokoya to the fevered, disturbed ground. Rider was pale and clammy, a flickering imprint in the Slack. Mokoya's graceless tensing through forest-nature told her nothing. The workings of the body, its branches and its energy flows, had always been opaque to her.

A lightcraft approached as Mokoya tracked the precarious contractions of Rider's heart. *One-two, one-two, one-two.* Her arms were shaking, her vision eaten by sparks of lightning.

"Nao?" She looked up. Thennjay was warm and solid against the dizzy, swallowing sky. She couldn't read his face, but she could read the alarm in his voice. "What have we gotten into, Nao?"

Mokoya pressed Rider to her bosom. She had no words for him.

# Chapter Eight

LIKE MOSS, LIFE SPILLED outward from Bataanar in the form of a hundred tents and caravans, where brown-toothed merchants and transients and others who couldn't find space within the tightly regulated city walls made camp and fought for scraps of whatever—food, trade, love—came their way.

It was here that Thennjay and his pugilists had un-furled their tents, choosing to put down their roots among the poor. The caravan city had escaped the brunt of the naga's attacks, and in one of the tents, Thennjay leaned over Rider's unconscious form, hands gentle on the pale damp of their forehead, working quietly through forest-nature.

Mokoya watched him while worrying at the bones of her hands, a thousand half-formed sentences swarming in her mind, drowning out all logical thought. Fragments of the past day tumbled loose in vivid flashes: The gray fabric of Rider's bed. The shadow of basalt outcrops in the desert. The explosion scars on Bataanar's walls, like black peonies. The sickening smell of burning flesh and oil—

No. That was a set of smells—and thoughts—from another time.

Thennjay stood. Through the ringing in her ears, Mokoya asked, "Well?"

His first answer skated past her in a collection of syllables that did not register as words. She blinked and forced herself to focus on the present. "What?"

With a gentle, patient air, Thennjay repeated, "No internal bleeding, no serious injuries. Just exhaustion. She'll recover."

"They."

"They," Thennjay acknowledged. He brushed fingers along the scars embroidering her face. "How about you?"

"I'll be fine."

He tilted his head. "All right." He had long years of experience, and he knew when it was futile to argue with Mokoya. He looked over at Rider. "Who are they?"

Mokoya told him what she knew. Her explanation, condensed to six sentences, sounded flimsy and inadequate. "That's all," she said at the end of it. "We've only just met."

"You like them," he said.

"I bedded them. It doesn't mean anything."

"You like them," he repeated, one corner of his lips lifting.

"Stop. I'm not *that* easy to read."

"Oh, my love." Thennjay laughed and caressed her cheek again. "You haven't changed."

She smiled back, then looked away. Beyond the cool dim flaps of the tent, a chorus of voices brawled and overlapped, but in here peace reigned. She felt herself settling in the present, her senses behaving better, her mind returning to roost.

The tent flaps rustled, and a stout, frowning entity pushed its way through. Adi. "Ah, you."

Patches of soot and rusty blood stained Adi's clothes. A thick, dark clot clung to her brow, but she waved off Thennjay's attempts to have a look. "Your friend's naga we tied outside with Phoenix," she said to Mokoya.

"Good. She's tame. She'll give you no trouble."

"Sure or not. She already tried to bite off Faizal's head."

"I don't blame her; sometimes I feel the same way."

Adi snorted, but her mirth was shallow. She shook her head. "Mokoya," she said, "we didn't sign up for this nonsense."

"I know. Adi, I won't blame you if you decide to go. I can't keep everyone safe."

"You see outside like that, how to go?" Adi let out a huge huff and planted her fists on her hips. "But you don't expect me to help with your politics."

"No. Of course not." As Adi turned to leave, she said, "Adi—thank you."

Adi ruched her nose. "You thank me for *what.*" And then she was gone.

"I love her," Thennjay said, in the space left by her departure.

It was just the two of them now, if you didn't count Rider. Adi's brief encroachment had brought back the gravity of the situation and the depth of the uncertainty they were mired in. Mokoya said, "What do you know about Tan Khimyan, the raja's advisor? What did Akeha tell you?"

"About her?" Thennjay shrugged. "Nothing, except that she interferes with all his plans, and he would like to acquaint her with a pit of vipers. You know how he is."

That didn't help Mokoya assemble a mental image of the woman, so she simply substituted the blank in her mind with a clone of her mother, equipped with the same face, the same mannerisms, and the same motivations. "She wants to destroy Bataanar. We have to stop her."

"Do we know that?" Thennjay drew in a huge breath, rotating his shoulders. "I'm not convinced she's controlling the naga. You saw it too. I don't know if that beast *can* be controlled."

Mokoya folded her arms. "That naga used slackcraft. You felt it, didn't you?" When Thennjay nodded reluctantly, she pressed on: "Animals don't become adepts—they're in no way complex enough. Something's been done to that naga. And that means whoever's experimented on it also developed a way of controlling it." She was definitely thinking of her mother now. "They wouldn't make a weapon they can't leash."

"Okay," Thennjay said. "Fair. But what if it's gone rogue?"

"Then we're not any less dead, are we?"

Thennjay shut his eyes, put his hands over his face, and sucked air through the gaps.

A familiar presence drew near, emerging from the swamp of activity around the tent. A narrow blade of focused purpose. She knew who it was before he came through the flaps. "Keha."

Sanao Akeha entered the tent with a frown, which was his default expression. The captain of Bataanar's city guard scanned the tiny, canvas-bound space, and the frown dissolved as he caught sight of his sister. "Moko. Thank the Almighty."

He crushed her in a hug, which she returned. Her twin stank of grease and dust and wood char, but he was alive and unhurt. She let go of the last dregs of resentment.

"*I* didn't get a hug," Thennjay grumbled.

Akeha remained unimpressed. "You didn't wipe her snot when she was six. Deal with it."

Mokoya elbowed Akeha in the chest, and he grunted. His gaze fell upon Rider's form on the bed. "Who's that?"

"A friend," Mokoya said, in the same moment Thennjay said, "Mokoya's new lover."

Akeha looked from one to the other. "All right." She saw him dismiss Rider as unimportant, a small but distracting pattern in one corner of a larger tapestry, and wanted to protest: *Wait, not so fast.*

But Thennjay was already moving the conversation onward. "Where's Yongcheow?"

"In the city. Trying to get Lady Han on the talker. Everything's gone to pieces around here." Akeha looked hollowed out. With proximity, Mokoya noticed how his hair hung in tangled clumps around his chin. Was that blood? She reached for it, and he batted her hand away.

Thennjay said, "We were discussing the naga before you arrived. We thought it might be under someone's control."

"That's wonderful. We've got bigger problems," Akeha said.

Mokoya squinted at him. "Bigger problems than that naga?"

His lips formed a grim line. "The raja has sent for Protectorate troops."

"That *fool.*" The words burst explosively from Thennjay. "After Bengang Baru? Did he learn nothing?"

Mokoya remembered Bengang Baru: a sleepy fishing

town with a small pewter factory, population five thousand. Unremarkable until it had accrued an unhealthy reputation as a Machinist hub. Officially, it had been flattened by a Machinist experiment gone wrong. But Mokoya had walked through the cratered, smoking streets, still hot and glowing with the bones of fisherfolk and the timbers of factory workers' houses, and she had seen the hand of the Protectorate everywhere. In the traces of slackcraft lingering still in the fire. In the wounds left in buildings by Protectorate guns. In the utter, ruthless devastation that was her mother's signature. No one had been left alive to tell the truth.

"You know Mother's just waiting for an excuse," Mokoya said. Protectorate troops would come not to defend, but to destroy. How could the raja be so stupid?

"His advisor has been trying to manufacture crises in the city for months now," Akeha growled. "Now she's finally got what she wanted."

"She's the one controlling the naga," Mokoya said. "I'm certain of that now." A narrative had lodged in the tracks of her mind. Tan Khimyan, disgraced Tensor, exiled to the wilds of Ea, seeking a way back to the capital. Decides to curry favor with the Protector by sacrificing a city—a Machinist base, after all, had to be destroyed, never mind the thousands who lived in it.

It was what Mother would do.

"We must ask him to rescind the call for aid," Thennjay said.

Akeha scowled. "Can you recall an arrow that has been fired?"

"What's the alternative?" Mokoya asked. "Sit around and wait for death?"

"Will I *sit around*? Are my people the type to simply *wait*?" Akeha countered, between his teeth. Fire burned in him, a gleam of light fixed on the spectacle of martyrdom.

"*Keha.*"

"Come on," Thennjay said, alarm gathering on his face. "We can't just prepare for the worst. *Come on.* We haven't even tried talking to the raja. We have to try." He looked at Akeha, as close to desperation as she'd ever seen him. "Just let me *try.*"

# Chapter Nine

BATAANAR WAS A CITY of curling streets, stacked with multilevel clay abodes and strung with shops that sold spices and fabric and hammered cook pots and cheap printed scrolls. The smell of roast meat and hot mutton fat hung over the outer quarters like a curtain. The three of them pushed their way toward the raja's palace in the center of the city, elbow to elbow with the thick unquiet of Bataanar's citizenry. First sunfall had come and gone, and the bazaars were wreathed in strings of sunballs, proper ones that dutifully gave off light and were unlikely to erupt in a volcanic pulse of heat and radiation.

The city had brushed off the morning's attack in the way cities with business to get to often do. Yet traces of emergency lingered. Conversations were subdued, contracted to the bare necessities of transaction. Merchants' wares huddled on carts and in boxes, ready to be whisked away at a moment's notice. Iron locusts patrolled the skies, hulking creatures of gray metal glowing with the raja's seal, broadcasting curfew instructions in four languages.

A sense of unease dogged Mokoya as she fell behind the other two. The gazes of shopkeepers and street vendors trailed her passage. Heavily wrapped women ducked their eyes at her approach and turned their heads once she walked past. Men, their hoods pulled tight around their heads, stared at her from side alleys and second-floor windows. Were they staring because they didn't know who she was? Or were they staring because they did? She had draped her cloak over the bright colors of the lizard arm, but the scars on her face were unmistakable. Her entire face was unmistakable.

She walked faster.

Laid over Bataanar's anxiety, Mokoya saw the ghost of Bengang Baru—the mutilated houses, the charred bones, the clogging, inescapable assault of putrefaction. The purge had happened six months ago, and she had pushed the memories deep into the quarantined districts of her mind. But it was all coming out of the ground again.

*A child-sized shoe lay by itself in the middle of a street, surrounded by destruction, its twin nowhere to be found. Its rim was stained sticky brown. Trying to imagine how it got there was worse than looking at the dead shells of houses. Somewhere Adi was calling her name, but all she could see was a foot ripped from an ankle, some scavenger coming by later to pry the flesh out of the shoe with sharp teeth—*

Mokoya desperately filled her lungs. The air in Bataanar was spiced with cinnamon, not decay. Under her breath, she whispered, "The Slack is all, and all is the Slack . . ."

Akeha turned around. "What was that?"

"Nothing."

Bataanar had ghosts of its own. Wherever she turned, there was the same picture—hung in gilt frames, draped with garlands, grayed by incense smoke—gracing the fronts of shops or peeping from their dimly lit interiors. An old portrait of the royal family. Raja Ponchak, smiling, ceremonially dressed, seated on a simple wooden chair with a plain gray backdrop. To the back and the left stood Raja Choonghey, tall and thin and sharp-faced. To the back and right was their daughter, Wanbeng, child-aged and apple-cheeked.

The girl would be eighteen now, Mokoya calculated, with the selfish and gut-shredding pang that accompanied thoughts of other people's daughters growing up.

Mokoya had met Raja Ponchak and her family only once: eight years ago, when the city had been consecrated, its streets neat and empty and the air still papery with construction dust. Thennjay had officiated the ceremony. She remembered very little of Raja Ponchak, except for the fragrant white buds she had worn in her hair that day. Of her husband Mokoya recalled even less. She did remember Wanbeng, who at ten years of age had developed an armor of aloofness. She had refused to play with Eien, whom she'd called "a baby who hasn't even picked their gender yet." Eien had been three years old.

It was strange walking through Bataanar and recognizing shards of its architecture—the splendid blue minarets of its grand mosque, the lines of its library tower—but having next to no memory of having visited. Intellectually she knew she had been here before, but a fundamental disconnect lay between her and the Mokoya who had accrued these impressions. That Mokoya had walked these pristine streets carrying her young child, probably laughing and thinking happy thoughts now opaque to her.

Maybe it was she who was the ghost.

The streets changed as they threaded deeper into Bataanar. The crowds diluted. The shops and open doors on the ground floors gave way to six-yield-high walls and barricaded gates. There the air was quieter and drained of smell. Buildings bulged like well-fed bellies, sporting arched windows and lamp-shaped cutouts on their walls. The streets sloped upward, more steeply at some points than others. Above them loomed the golden teardrop domes of the royal palace.

The raja's palace was a series of round, white-walled stone buildings. A wide swath of extravagantly watered garden surrounded the compound, ardently lit and fragrant in the desert air. At its edge waited a statuesque figure: a woman with thick arms and a face that could light dreams. Her robes were that of a high-placed servant's, simple, but well kept. Kebang? Mahanagay? Mokoya wasn't sure.

Akeha hissed when she saw her. "Get out of here, Silbya. You can't block us from seeing the raja."

"I have no intention of doing so," she said. "My mistress wishes to extend an invitation for an audience with Tensor Sanao." She looked at Mokoya and made a small gesture of obeisance. "Tensor. My mistress, the raja's advisor—"

"Tan Khimyan," Mokoya said. The expression on Akeha's face had told her everything she needed. A brief spurt of adrenaline ran through her. "What does she want with me?"

Silbya carried herself with calm and simplicity. "She has some matters she wishes to discuss. What they are, I cannot disclose."

Thennjay was looking at her in alarm. Akeha's lips curled in distaste. But the emotion that poured through Mokoya burned like fire and felt like the hunger of a tiger smelling prey. She wanted to face this woman and stare her in the eyes.

"I'll go," she said. Beside her, Akeha reacted with consternation, imperceptible to all but her. She squeezed his arm.

As children in the Grand Monastery, they had perfected a way of speaking directly through the Slack. Akeha looked fiercely into her eyes, and she quieted her mindeye to listen.

*She's dangerous,* he said. *Watch where your feet land. Try not to die on me.*

*Don't be an idiot,* she replied. *Of course I'll be careful.* But she thought that it was the advisor who should be careful.

# Chapter Ten

THE ADVISOR'S RESIDENCE STOOD in the middle of a massive paved courtyard, surrounded by gold-embellished white walls. The tops of trees could be seen within the compound walls: graceful swoops of willow, spikes of cherry blossom, heavy boughs of tamarind. The door, thick and red and punctuated by round gold studs, was guarded by a man and a woman in quilted Protectorate armor.

Mokoya followed Silbya's unwavering path. The woman had not spoken on their trip up here, a sealed vessel from whom Mokoya could glean nothing. Mokoya had spent the time mouthing the First Sutra under her breath in a vain attempt to keep her heart rate steady.

"We are expected," Silbya told the guards. The woman tugged on the Slack to open the doors.

Gravel paths forded thick rich soil. Peony bushes bloomed amongst the trees. The red arch of a wooden bridge graced a fishpond, where a pair of palm-sized terrapins sunned themselves. At the end of the garden stood the advisor's house, dark timber columns supporting a peaked roof threaded from corner to corner with carven dragons.

It looked and smelled like home.

Mokoya entered the advisor's receiving chamber to the sounds of strife. A voice, fortified by the arrogance of youth, rang out: "You can take your *false* concern and put it up your own *behind*."

Princess Wanbeng and Tan Khimyan were locked in verbal battle at the center of a cavernous room decked with shadows. Hanging trees and thick vines climbed golden frames that lined the chamber. In the back a fine silver mesh caged swooping flocks of birds and a sleek pile of breathing, growling fur: a tiger, eyes yellow, paws huge and idle. A hand thrust into a slash in the wires would never emerge again.

"Princess," said Tan Khimyan, "your lack of decorum will not serve you well in Chengbee."

"Good, because I'm *not* going to Chengbee."

Wanbeng had the solid, corded look of a person who spent her days running and climbing. The child in the framed pictures had grown into a formidable young woman. Her hair was gathered high in an efficient bun, and she wore a closed, disdainful expression.

And there was Tan Khimyan, the woman Mokoya had imagined as identical to her mother. The reality was deflating. A small, pale-skinned woman with narrow features, she was not half as physically imposing as Mother. Worse still, she lacked the Protector's presence, instead appearing to be overwhelmed by her ornate surroundings, like a child playing at being important. Disappointment set in. Contempt, even.

Tan Khimyan said to Wanbeng, "My dear child, think of your poor father. This is his wish for you."

"I care *nothing* for his wishes. When Mother was dying, did he care for mine? No, he did *not*."

Tan Khimyan sighed. "As you grow up, you will come to find that you should treasure your father's intentions. He means the best for you." She looked at Mokoya, the first acknowledgment that she had seen her guest. "I'm sure the Tensor here agrees."

Mokoya raised an eyebrow. "Best intentions? My own mother bore me because she owed the Grand Monastery a blood debt. Are those the best intentions you mean?"

Wanbeng smirked. Seemingly emboldened by Mokoya's statement, she said, "Here is what I think of my father's *best intentions*." She pulsed through water-nature. Glass shattered; on the long workbench that occupied the left side of the chamber, fragile objects cascaded to the ground. Boiling vessels, pipettes, and jars of chemicals burst into glittering fireworks. A hundred thousand weapons with which to cut the skin, to impale the self.

Tan Khimyan's face went tight, and Mokoya watched her knuckles press through the skin of her hands. *Weak,* she thought. *Mother would eat her alive. No wonder she was expelled from the city.*

It had been years, and still her mother's way of thinking crept through her mind like an elusive, fleeting specter. She shivered.

"Don't waste my time again," Wanbeng said, and she spun on her heel to leave.

"Silbya," Tan Khimyan said, her voice straining against spikes of emotion, "come clear this up."

The woman obeyed without a word. Tan Khimyan turned to Mokoya, and her face shifted into a diplomat's smile. "My apologies, Tensor. Come, let us retire to a more civilized location."

Tan Khimyan vanished into the shadows on the right. Mokoya stepped after her, but when she glanced back, she saw Wanbeng brazenly lift a small jade carving from one of Tan Khimyan's display shelves and pocket it.

She admired the girl's boldness, at least.

Tan Khimyan took her to a large study lit by silk-screened windows. A carved desk and tall-backed chair in matching rosewood lorded over the middle of the room. The desk hosted a tea set, an inkpot, brushes, and a pile of scrolls, arranged into a neat pattern with religious precision.

"Would you like some tea, Tensor Sanao? I've been looking forward to this day for a while now."

"Is that so?"

"Of course." She made her way around her desk and picked up the teapot without waiting for Mokoya's answer.

Tan Khimyan dressed her shapely form in finely fitted silk. Her hair, sculpted to arboreal intricacy, glittered with the insectile weight of jewels. Mokoya had almost forgotten the fanciful ways women in the capital were expected to paint their faces, the rouge for the cheeks and lips, the stone-ink in place of eyebrows. She didn't appreciate this reminder.

"Children these days," Tan Khimyan remarked. "More like wild horses than civilized beings. Wanbeng's been a thorn in her father's eye for quite some time now. She is of the age to further her education, but she is reluctant to leave the provincial lands she grew up in. She will come around. She is a sensible child, after all."

Mokoya noticed the cushion on the floor in front of the desk. Two ovals on the shiny surface of the fabric had been worn gray by the knees of countless supplicants. "I don't expect you to kneel, of course," Tan Khimyan said. "That's for the workers. You are different."

"How magnanimous of you." Mokoya wasn't sure the sarcasm in her voice came through.

"I always thought it a pity that I was not an advisor in Bataanar when you last visited," Tan Khimyan said, as she washed the teacups. "We could have met then. But of course, many things have changed since that time."

Mokoya met her prattle with a wall of silence. She did not take the teacup when it was offered to her, and Tan Khimyan put the cup away with a peeved expression. She was so easily pushed.

Mokoya said, "Did you summon the naga to the city?"

Tan Khimyan sighed and settled on the edge of her desk with the weight of a brocaded curtain. "You're a plain talker, I see. All right." She crossed one knee over the other. "In the interest of honesty, I shall tell you: I did not."

Mokoya snorted.

"You may find it hard to believe. But this is true. I had a hand in creating the beast, but someone else is controlling it."

"So you admit to creating the naga?"

She shrugged. "I see no point in concealing that fact from you. Yes, Tensor, I admit it. I was part of the group in Chengbee that created this naga." A dry, humorless chuckle followed. "It was what caused my exile from the capital, after all."

Mokoya wasn't buying it. "If you're not the one summoning the naga, who is? Who else knows it exists?"

"Who, indeed?" The silky way she said it insisted she had an answer.

Her posturing was starting to grate on Mokoya's nerves. "Speak plainly."

"Think a little, Tensor, and the answer will become clear. You've met her."

Mokoya squinted. "Who, Wanbeng?" Sarcasm masked panic: she didn't understand Tan Khimyan's insinuation, and a fear of losing the conversation's thread swelled in her.

Tan Khimyan exhaled and capitulated. Mokoya's unintended feint had worked. "I speak of Swallow."

"Swallow?" A name? A bird?

Another deep sigh. "This coyness benefits neither of us, Tensor." As cold water filled Mokoya's spine like river water, she said, "Everyone's seen the Quarterlandish girl who fights by your side. It's hard to miss someone who rides a naga mount."

*Swallow.* The name was wrong, and the pronouns were wrong, but Tan Khimyan was referring to Rider. Rider, who lay unconscious in a tent outside the city. Rider, who had the ability to draw unwarranted smiles out of Mokoya.

Tan Khimyan stood and began a circuit of her desk. "I brought you here to warn you of her duplicity. I can tell Swallow has wormed her way into your good graces. But you must not make the mistake of trusting her, as I did."

Mokoya shifted weight between her feet, not sure what to do with her hands, which had begun to prickle as if insects writhed inside her fingers.

"You may not know her very well, but we were to-gether for many years. I took her in, I sheltered her, and I protected her in the capital. For all that, she betrayed me. That's the kind of person she is."

"Betrayed you?"

"She was the one who reported our experiments. Did she not tell you?"

No, of course Rider had told her. Things slipped her mind so easily these days. Mokoya folded her arms to hide the fact that they were shaking. "I have only your word that she's responsible."

"Ah, Tensor. I wish I had proof to offer you! But the fortunes are not so kind. All I have is circumstantial evidence."

Mokoya took the bait: "What evidence?"

"A few months ago, my chambers were broken into. All my notes about the experiment went missing. They are everything someone would need to control the naga. The guards saw no one come in or leave. And they're quite thorough, my guards. Silbya would know if the compound was breached." She looked seriously at Mokoya. "Now, can you think of anyone you know who has the ability to travel from place to place without being detected? Someone who can bend the Slack?"

Mokoya's pulse accelerated. "Any thief with the right

skills could have broken into your quarters undetected. Your so-called evidence means nothing."

"But it's Swallow. I'm sure of it. It could be no one else."

"That's easy for you to say."

All attempts at posturing had fled Tan Khimyan. What remained was iron-jawed determination and a refusal to look away from Mokoya, who found the fish-spear attention unnerving.

"Listen, Tensor," Tan Khimyan said. "I know we have no reason to be friends. Certainly your brother, for all that we have clashed, would have set you against me." With broad strides, she closed the gap between them, reaching for Mokoya. "But Bataanar is my home now. And I will not see it destroyed."

Mokoya took a step back, away from the woman's grasping hands. Colorful emotions burned through the arm hidden by her cloak.

"Look through her belongings. Find what she has stolen from me. That'll be all the evidence you need."

"I don't understand. Why would they do this?"

"Swallow? She seeks revenge, Tensor. She would see me utterly destroyed. It was not enough for her to have me turned out of my life and my home. She will plague me into the grave."

Mokoya thought of the night they'd spent together,

recalling Rider's strangeness and intensity, tempered by great curiosity and great warmth. She had believed in that warmth, had found comfort in it, had briefly relied upon it as a fount of human compassion. When she tried to picture them bearing the kind of grudge Tan Khimyan was accusing them of, her mind stumbled over the jagged incongruity.

The woman studied Mokoya's reaction. At least she had stopped trying to touch Mokoya; she had realized it would end badly. "You still don't believe me, of course. But you have known her only briefly. I suspect you'll learn better."

Mokoya thought, *You can't even use the right pronouns for them. You don't even know their real name.*

And then: *How do I know that I know their real name?*

She shivered. Was she sure she knew Rider better than this woman did? Would she be willing to bet Bataanar's fate on it?

~

When Mokoya left Tan Khimyan's residence, the distant, rational part of her mind said she needed to find Akeha and Thennjay. But her feet were already taking her down the narrow path back through Bataanar, back through the suffocating heat, back through the staring, distrustful crowds. All of it—the noise, the shoving, the smells of sweat and cooking—came in through a thick filter. They were sensations being picked up by someone else's body, in which she was only a guest.

She dutifully put one foot in front of the other and kept breathing.

The tent city was prefaced by Bramble's sloping form. The naga rested on the cooling sand with Phoenix tucked under one blue-and-yellow wing. The raptor jumped up in a flurry of delight when she saw Mokoya, but her excitement dampened as Mokoya stroked her nose. She knew something was wrong.

"Shh," Mokoya said, as Phoenix pressed her massive head into her hands and whined.

Bramble growled and rustled her wings, watching Mokoya carefully. The naga was less skittish than she had been before—Phoenix's presence seemed to calm her down. It was a pity. The two of them appeared to be getting along so well.

Rider was alive, awake, and crouched over something when Mokoya entered the tent. They jumped up, and a flash of emotion—shock or guilt, or both—crossed their face. "Mokoya."

The tent looked like a typhoon had hit it. Someone had brought Mokoya's belongings in from the desert and left them in haphazard clumps. Boxes and small bags lay around, and they all looked like they had been opened. A stack of journals sat on top of the box Mokoya had put them in. Anger tore through her gut. "Have you been looking through my things?"

That look of guilt again. "Yes. *No.*" Color flushed through Rider's pale cheeks. "The crew brought your things in—there was a flash storm in the desert while you were in the city. We wanted to make sure nothing had water damage."

If truth had a shape, her words fit its boundaries. A wash of petrichor had weighted the air outside, which she had mistaken for oasis smell. Heavy clashes of slack-craft could, and often would, disrupt weather patterns.

Still the sense of violation remained. "You read my journals?"

"I did not." Their brows furrowed. "I would never do such a thing without your consent, Mokoya."

One of the capture pearls sat by itself on top of an up-turned crate. Mokoya frowned at it, and Rider noticed. "Mokoya," they said placatingly, reaching for her arm. Their fingers froze an inch from her skin, as if they were afraid to make contact.

"You looked through that one," she said.

"I—" Their shoulders cramped into an apologetic shape. "I was merely curious—I wanted to study the technique behind it. I did not know they contained your personal memories. I am sorry, Mokoya."

Heavy browns and greens swirled in the belly of the capture pearl like swamp water. Mokoya knew which it was by sight. It contained her last argument with Thennjay, captured for posterity: the Grand Monastery in the grip of a heat wave, Phoenix showered by dying cherry blossoms, Mokoya tying her scattershot possessions to the raptor's back.

*"Stay? With a man who's given up on our daughter?"*

*"Eien is dead, Nao. She's gone. You have to accept that."*

*"She's gone, but we haven't lost her."*

*"Phoenix is just a copy. Nao! She's not going to bring Eien back."*

*Pulling on the reins, ropes biting into her skin. "Good-bye, Thenn."*

"Mokoya?"

She blinked. The capture pearl was gripped in her shaking hands, even though she had no memory of picking it up. The vision of Chengbee in the dying summer faded from around her. She felt like a chunk of time had been ripped from her, leaving a hollow in her body.

Rider looked afraid, but whether they were afraid of Mokoya or afraid for her, she couldn't tell. "I apologize, Mokoya. If I had known, I would not have touched it."

Mokoya's fingers spasmed as she put the capture pearl back down. She had to force words through the clot of tension stoppering her chest. "Why does Tan Khimyan call you *Swallow*?"

Rider's eyes widened. "Have you met her?"

She let the frost in her manner answer.

Rider intently surveyed the mess on the ground. "That was the name she gave me. She disliked the one I have." They fidgeted like they wanted to tidy away the chaos, but didn't dare to. "What did she say about me?"

"She said *you* were the one summoning the naga. She said you stole her notes. She said you'll destroy Bataanar in your vendetta against her."

Rider froze, then moved away so that Mokoya couldn't see their reaction. Quietly they said, "So that is the story that she has woven, is it? Ah, Khimyan."

The words were tainted with a filamentous tenderness Mokoya couldn't parse. They turned back around. "How disappointing. I was not expecting this from her."

"Are you denying this? You're telling me she's lying?"

"What part of that story sounds true to you?"

Mokoya folded her arms. "Whoever stole her notes broke into her compound without alerting the guards. It sounds like something you'd be capable of doing."

"I would be *capable of doing*?" As Rider repeated her words, Mokoya realized how harsh they sounded, but it was too late. They had already left her mouth like a cloud of poison gas.

The guilt must have made its way to her face, because Rider said, "You are not to blame, Mokoya. After all, you know very little of me." Hesitantly, they moved closer to her. "What can I do to ease your suspicions? Would you like to examine my belongings? It would prove I do not possess what she accuses me of taking."

Mokoya sucked in a breath. A logical person would say, *Yes, let's do that. Let's put aside all doubts.* But the hurt she'd glimpsed on Rider's face left a lingering chill. She felt that agreeing to this would put a permanent wall of mistrust between them. Any hope of a normal relationship would be crushed under its weight.

So she resisted. She dug her heels in against the pull of logic. She said, against her better instincts, "You don't have to do that. I trust you." A hundred starlings took flight in her chest as she mouthed the words.

Her declaration didn't lift Rider's mood as she had expected. If anything, the frown on their face deepened. "Do you? Why?"

"I trust you more than I trust Tan Khimyan," she said, and that part was true as the sun's path across the sky. "Besides," she said, as the thought occurred to her, "her theory doesn't hold weight. Like you told me, you need to put in an anchor point to travel long distances."

"Yes, that is true," Rider said slowly, latching on to her idea. "Not knowing what lies inside her compound, I would not risk folding in without an anchor. Not even if I were close by."

Yes. Mokoya felt foolish. The facts were so clear, she felt embarrassed for not realizing this earlier. But Tan Khimyan had unnerved her so much, she hadn't been thinking straight. She recalled the geography of the woman's receiving chamber, with all its death traps, and a small laugh burst free. "She's got a tiger in a cage. A blind jump would be a terrible idea."

Rider reacted with a spark of recognition. "A tiger? Oh, I cannot believe she brought Khun with her. Poor Khun! He hated the summer. He must be miserable in this heat." They leaned into Mokoya's inner space, sharp and curious. "How does he fare? He was barely out of cubhood when I left."

"He's definitely not a cub now. He would probably swallow you in four bites. If you happened to jump into his cage, that is."

And finally, Rider smiled. The discomfort between them washed away in the light of that small gesture. Mokoya felt her nerves ease for the first time since she'd entered the tent. What a fool she had been. Rider had risked their life to protect Bataanar. They had fought the naga together. Why had she believed Tan Khimyan in the first place?

Rider's fingers brushed against her fringe, tracing

topographies on the gnarled skin of her cheek. "Are you well, Mokoya? The past day has been hard on you."

She chuckled lightly and pulled them into a gentle embrace. "I've had worse days. And I'm glad you've recovered."

Rider sucked on their lower lip and coyly said, "I could show you how well I've recovered, if you like."

Mokoya laughed and let Rider kiss her. But she made sure the kiss was contained and kept firm her grip on Rider's hands so they weren't tempted to slip past the point of no return. "I can't, not now. I need to talk to my brother."

# Chapter Eleven

SECOND-SUNRISE GLIMMERED in the sky as Mokoya plunged back into Bataanar's labyrinthine anatomy. The city's public spaces were hemorrhaging people under the pressure of the raja's sunup curfew, and she found herself a solitary figure wandering the hollow bones of streets, with only an occasional straggler and a circulation of iron locusts, looming and vigilant, to keep her company. Stripped of life, the white walls of the city appeared bleached by the brightening sun.

Across the city from the oasis gate, the main royal guardhouse perched on the eastern city wall, a squat edifice of dull brick protruding from the fortifications. Mokoya's way up was barred by two of the city guard, set across the bottom of the stairwell. Both of them were tall as she was, and half again as broad.

"Entry is forbidden," said the one on the left, a woman.

"You shouldn't be out here anyway," said the one on the right. He looked too young to be holding a job like this. "There's a curfew on."

"I'm here to see my brother," Mokoya said, impatient. "Your captain."

Confusion blurred the boy guard's syllables. "We don't allow family visits—"

"Zak, wait." His colleague frowned at Mokoya, studying the planes of her face, the broad collection of scars. "Right, you *are* Captain Sanao's sister, I'll believe that. But we weren't told to expect anyone."

"I just spoke to Akeha on the talker, not a half hour ago. He knows I'm coming." This was a fucking waste of time. She thought about cracking their skulls together and leaving them heaped at the bottom of the stairs. She might, if they delayed her further.

"Let me check," the woman said.

She pushed back a sleeve, exposing the voice transmitter strapped to her wrist. Mokoya blinked. It was an open secret that the city guard sheltered the Machinist rebellion in Bataanar, but parading Machinist technology under the raja's nose was a fresh, trenchant show of boldness.

The woman tapped the transmitter. Metallic noise screeched from it before Akeha's voice surged through, thick with irritation: "What is it now?"

"It's Lao. Your sister's h—"

"Is your head rotting? Send her up. Stop wasting my time."

The signal dropped like a man with his throat cut. Lao smiled thinly at Mokoya. "Well. You heard the boss."

He hadn't let her finish a third word. That was impressive, even for Akeha. The meeting with the raja must not have gone well.

In the gloom at the top of the stairs stood the guardroom door, metal-boned and solid in its frame. Mokoya pushed it open.

Light and chaos swallowed her.

If the transmitter had been a brazen display of Machinist affiliation, Mokoya was stepping into the beating, brawling heart of that daring. The guardroom boiled with enclosed sweat and steam, heated by glass balls of light that hung from an overhead forest of wires. Machine schematics papered the walls. Fifty-odd faces turned to stare at her, distracted from their tasks: Stacking boxes. Opening boxes. Screen-printing circulars. At one long table, about ten people sat, halfway through assembling and polishing guns.

Over this manifold scene of arrested productivity towered the biggest generator Mokoya had ever seen, a gourd-shaped bronze furnace on a triplet of clawed legs, attended to by a forest of thick pipes. The air in the room surged tidally as it thrummed and purred, a breath cycle to rival a naga's.

Mokoya looked at the burnt patina of lilac bruises on

the generator's skin, imagined pressing the flesh of her wrists against it, and shuddered through a memory of the Grand Monastery in the seconds before the explosion.

"Nao! You're alive."

The present day called. Around a table overflowing with scrolls and journals stood Thennjay and Akeha, their calculated distance and folded arms calcified around an argument she had missed.

"Yes," she said. "Yes, I am."

Behind the table's accrued detritus sat Yongcheow, one foot propped up on his stool, flipping through a journal with determined nonchalance.

"What did Tan Khimyan want from you?" Akeha asked.

"Nothing important. She tried to blame Rider for the naga attack. She thought I might believe her."

He squinted. "Who's Rider?"

"My friend. In the tent."

She could tell that Akeha had forgotten who they were, and she took vindictive pleasure at his internal struggle. *Serves him right for not paying attention.* She pressed forward, sidestepping his discomfort: "What's happening now?"

Akeha shook his head as he resurfaced. "What does it look like?" During their conversation, the guardroom had returned to swarming industriousness. Somebody hammered at something, a sound of wood against metal. In the background, the generator hummed and clicked. It was very loud.

"He's preparing for war," Thennjay said.

*He.* Not *we.* "You'd prefer to do something else," she said.

Akeha, talking over Thennjay, gibed: "He'd prefer we bang our foreheads against a wall until they bleed."

"Bengang Baru only happened because its mayor helped," Thennjay insisted. Mokoya recognized his tone; it was the one he used in quarrels he'd already lost a dozen times. "We could still turn things around here."

In between them, fixated on pages of his journal, Yongcheow muttered, "I still think we should be prepared in case the naga comes back."

"It won't come back," Akeha snapped. "Tan Khimyan has gotten what she wants. The troops are already on their way. Why would she need another attack?"

Yongcheow shrugged. "It would be better if we fixed that shield. Surely you can spare an engineer or two."

"Who would then be wasting time repairing it, instead of making sure everybody has weapons that work."

Yongcheow shrugged again. He flipped a page.

Was it her imagination, or had the generator's clicking grown louder? She turned her head to listen. She swore its mechanical aspiration had sped up.

Thennjay said, "Akeha, preparing for a street battle is a mistake. It's going to be a bloodbath."

"What choice do I have? The Protectorate comes in two days. And Choonghey won't change his mind. Don't be a fool." One of his guards stood shiftily by the side, clutching a scroll in her hands. Akeha waved her over.

"I told you we've focused on the wrong person," Thennjay said, as Akeha inspected the list the girl presented him. "He's an old man. Old men are like donkeys: they're stubborn, and they'll kick you every chance they get. We need to talk to his daughter. Use her to influence him."

"The oasis gate needs more medics," Akeha told his underling. "Ask Anh to see if there might be more volunteers from the clans." As she hurried off, he turned on Thennjay. "You want to *use* an eighteen-year-old girl?"

"She's old enough."

"Old enough for what?"

The clicking was definitely louder. The surge, recede, surge, recede of the thrumming accelerated in pace with her heartbeat. It was going to blow. She couldn't save them all. She wouldn't move fast enough to fling herself in between. Maybe she could make a barrier, throw it around Akeha and Thennjay. Maybe she should make that barrier, right now. Now, before—

"Nao? What is it?"

Her heart stopped in her chest, then started again. They were looking at her, all three of them, and she realized they were waiting for her answer. What had they been discussing? Something about Wanbeng. Something like, if she failed and there was war and hundreds died, how would she feel? Something.

Numbness sparked through her hands, paralyzed her tongue. She found movement from somewhere and said, "Wanbeng is no wilting flower. We should talk to her." Her voice wobbled, but at least the words that came out of her were human.

Akeha looked at her longer than necessary. Then he allowed himself a long, angry sigh. "*Fine*. Go chase your water mirages. Leave me alone to do the real work."

She said, to his petulant outburst, "What's the harm in talking to her?"

Akeha's only response was to storm away. He gestured to another of his guards and began speaking to him, his back turned to them, his words too low to make out.

There was no point arguing with Akeha when he got in a mood. Mokoya touched Thennjay's arm lightly. "Let's go."

Thennjay turned to follow her, but when she'd pushed the guardroom door open, Akeha's voice rang out over the clamor. "If it were your daughter, would you say *what's the harm?*"

Mokoya's lips curled as the question hit like a punch, but it was Thennjay who growled, "You dare?"

Akeha's face flickered with unreadable emotion. Mokoya tugged at Thennjay. "Come." There was no use in lingering further.

# Chapter Twelve

**THE SUN LURCHED THROUGH** the pale sky as they threaded through the empty shells of Bataanar's streets. Second-sunfall wouldn't be for another hour yet. Mokoya linked her arm with Thennjay's, the yellow of her skin changing spectrum against his warmth.

Thennjay was silent, letting the heaviness of his footsteps and the uncharacteristic shallowness of his breath speak for him. Mokoya, squeezing his arm, allowed him his solitude. Her husband hardly ever talked about how Eien's death affected him. In the tangle of months following the accident, he had been the calm center in the storm of Mokoya's emotions, holding on to her as she raged and fought. It was easy to believe that he had simply risen above the base nature of humanity. Easy to believe that he, in his meditative way, had peacefully accepted what the fortunes had dealt him.

It had infuriated her. She wanted him to grieve as she had grieved. She would lash out at him, throw breakable items, call him heartless, monstrous. But she never managed to shatter his calm.

In the years that passed after she left him for a vagrant's life, she'd had time to consider what those first few weeks must have been like for him: his child dead and his wife lying in a sickbed, fighting not to follow after her. After she recovered, he would often take her right hand and squeeze it, whether in bed or in the middle of an argument. At the time, she'd thought it was meant to comfort her, but she wasn't the one who'd needed comforting. Mokoya pictured the way it had become reflex in the days he stood over her broken body and counted her breaths. How he would touch the flesh of her right arm, because as long as her body was accepting the new graft, it wasn't dying.

Sometimes she would wonder: Did he cry? Or did he keep his emotions bound, as always?

"What really happened when you met Tan Khimyan?" he asked.

Bataanar became solid brick around her once more. "I told you," she said. "She accused Rider of calling the naga to the city."

"And you don't believe her, do you?"

She remembered the conversation in the tent and the comforting conviction she had mustered. "Of course not. I trust Rider."

"All right," Thennjay said. "I'll believe that."

"What is this about, Thenn?"

"Back in the guardroom, you went somewhere else. Something really upset you. I thought it might have been Tan Khimyan."

"No. It's just . . ." *Everything,* she wanted to say. "The past two days have been very stressful. You do remember today's the anniversary, don't you?"

"Yes, Nao," he said patiently. "I do."

At least there was a specific trigger for the guardroom incident. "It was the generator," she explained. "Its size, and the noise . . ." The ache of panic lingered in her chest, even with time and space insulating her from that room. Trying to ease Thennjay's worry, she added, "Generators don't usually affect me like this. It was just this one, and with everything that's been going on . . ."

"Oh, Nao." He tightened his grip on her arm.

Led by Thennjay, they kept a steady pace, each step crossing one of the flat rectangular tiles that made up Bataanar's roads. With the curfew still on, it felt like the two of them were the only things left alive in the world.

"I'm not well," she finally admitted, setting free the swarm of locusts that had nested inside her for far too long. "I thought I would return to the monastery when I got better. But I'm not getting any better. I'm afraid all the time, I can't control my thoughts. I don't know how long I can go on like this."

Thennjay said nothing. Just listened.

She said, "You know what's the worst part?"

His voice was soft. "What is, Nao?"

"I miss having prophecies." She shook her head. "All my life I resented them. I hated being shown things and knowing I couldn't change them. Now? I want them back. At least I could be *sure* of my prophecies."

Thennjay walked a few steps in silence. "Do you think they'll ever return to you?"

"No. I don't know." Something stirred in the depths of her consciousness, a memory of something odd. Mokoya's steps slowed as she pulled on that murky thread, trying to reel in the thought attached to it. "Rider said something strange to me when they were teaching me to fold the Slack. They thought I had been *actively* seeking out prophecies."

"Did you tell them the truth?"

"I did. And they left it alone. But it was a shocking thing to hear. As if I'd made a choice not to have them anymore."

Mokoya's thoughts rolled further than her words dared to. When she'd folded the Slack earlier, she'd been stunned by how easily it came to her. It felt almost like muscle memory, as though she were echoing something she'd done all her life.

An ice-water thought washed over her and cascaded down her spine. What if she could, in fact, choose where and when to see the prophecies?

Thennjay had turned down a different path of thought. "Are you sure you'd *want* the ability to control them?"

She had no answer to that.

As they came in sight of the raja's palace, Thennjay said, "Nao. If you want something to be sure of, I can give you one."

She met his gaze, and there was infinite tenderness in it. "The monastery will always be open to you," he said. "And you will find me waiting there. Always. No matter how long it takes."

~

"I don't know what you think I can do," Princess Wanbeng declared. "And I don't know why you think I'd do it." With her white-clad back to them, it was impossible to make out the girl's expression, but the contempt in her voice made that unnecessary.

"This concerns the fate of Bataanar," Thennjay said. "This city is your home. You must care about it, even just a little bit."

Princess Wanbeng's room occupied the top floor of the library tower, drowned in light pouring from stone-carved windows the right size and height to jump out of. High above them sat a dome of mountain glass. Woven with slackcraft, the glass was clear under starlight, and hard and opaque as mortar when the sun rose. Shelves and bookcases cluttered the circular room, whose contents told nothing of the owner save that she cared nothing for order and that she liked horses.

On their way up the tower, Thennjay and Mokoya had been stopped by an apologetic pair of palace guards. The princess wouldn't be seeing anyone at the moment, they'd said. She was not well.

They had been close enough to the top that sounds echoed downward: somebody shouting. Mokoya had recognized Wanbeng's voice. "Is the princess with someone?" she'd asked.

The guards' nervous discretion had yielded under further questioning, trepidation and worry intertwined in the answers: No, she was alone. The princess sometimes talked to herself. She'd never really recovered from her mother's death, see. It had gotten worse in the last few months, yes.

Now the girl was using distance as shield, keeping as much of it between them as possible. Her hands fluttered, occupied in moving scrolls and readers from one pile to another. "Oh. Yes. The fate of Bataanar. Because your *precious* Machinists believe the Protectorate spews death everywhere it goes. Destruction."

"We have genuine reasons to believe that the troops

*will* purge Bataanar," Thennjay said. "Whatever his distaste for Machinists, your father can't possibly desire a massacre of his people." His manner was slow, honey-smooth, and diplomatic in a way Mokoya could never be.

But it was pointless. Wanbeng continued with her haphazard tidying, Thennjay's overtures bouncing off the wall of her indifference. Eventually, she turned to face them. "Fine. Let's make a bargain. I'll talk to Father, *if* you do a favor for me." As Thennjay opened his mouth to speak, she cut him off. "Not you. *Her.*"

Mokoya could imagine her mother being like this at eighteen. Her enchantment with the girl had faded fast. She folded her arms. "What kind of favor?"

Wanbeng's tone was calculating. "You're a Tensor."

"They never revoked my membership, so yes, I suppose I am."

"Good. Then you should know that two months ago I was accepted into the Tensorate academy."

Mokoya frowned. The Tensorate academy accepted barely a hundred students each year, and commoners could spend a lifetime taking the admission exams and fail every time. But Wanbeng was nobility, and her father had already been a high-ranking official in the Protectorate before he married Raja Ponchak. Of course she would be accepted.

Thennjay said, "Congratulations. Your father must be very proud."

Wanbeng's stuttering laugh sounded like a string of firecrackers going off. "Of *course* he is. It was what *he* wanted."

"You don't sound happy about it," Mokoya said.

"Happy? *Happy?* Did anyone ask what would make me happy? No. I want my acceptance rescinded. Tensor Sanao, this is your half of the bargain."

"You don't want to enter the academy," Mokoya said, slow comprehension—adjacent to sympathy—descending upon her.

The girl folded her arms. "I would rather *die* than go. Who wants to live in Chengbee? I don't know *anyone* there."

When Mokoya was eighteen, her mother had said, *I'll only let you marry him if you go to the Academy. This is non-negotiable.* Oh, she understood what Wanbeng felt. Yet: "I can't do what you ask."

The girl's white teeth showed like darts. "You're the Protector's daughter, aren't you? Anything you want, you just have to ask. *Nobody* will refuse you!"

Mokoya's lip curled sardonically. "You don't understand the situation at all, do you?" She preferred to spare children from the barbs of her sarcasm, but if this one thought she had any sway left with the apparatus of the

Protectorate—well. She could have been far more scathing.

Wanbeng looked first at her, then at Thennjay, before she shrugged and smiled. "Then I won't talk to Father. Go away."

The words were childish, and from the casual way she said them, Mokoya realized Wanbeng wasn't truly concerned about the academy at all. The girl was deflecting, aimlessly moving troops around on the board until they went away.

Still Thennjay persisted as Wanbeng turned back to shifting things from one pointless location to the other. "Wanbeng, this isn't a game. Thousands of people could die if we do nothing."

No response. The girl's gaze was fixed on a particularly haphazard pile: stacked scrolls mixed with paper codices and loose sheaves annotated with ink. Her fingertips drummed on the desk surface.

There had to be something she could be pushed to care about.

Mokoya said, "Do it for your mother's sake, if nothing else."

Wanbeng spun as though Mokoya's words had been a firebrand. "Don't talk to me about my mother," she hissed. "You *don't*, you—" Her voice grew tight, then faltered. Her hands curled into weapons. *"Get out."*

Something was off. Mokoya had expected grief from her, or anger. But it was guilt and fear that had taken hold of her face.

Thennjay remained stubborn, jumping onboard Mokoya's pivot. "Wanbeng," he said, "We knew your mother. The welfare of the city was her first priority—"

"You know *nothing*," Wanbeng said. Seismic stress filled her voice. She was only eighteen, and the fragility of her youth was showing. "*Nothing* about her life, or her *death*, or—" She sucked in a breath. "You met my mother once. You never *knew* her."

During this tirade, Mokoya's eyes had fallen on one of the long, thin desks. Recognition knifed through her ribs at the same time she wondered why she hadn't noticed it earlier. Resting on the pile of writings on Wanbeng's desk was a beautiful, perfectly geometrical object. A coruscating, hollow dodecahedron, covered in delicate figurines of the zodiac in repose.

Everything else fell away. "What is that?" Mokoya asked, pointing, even though she knew the answer.

Wanbeng stepped in front of the desk defensively, as if to block it from Mokoya's view, as if she could distract Mokoya into forgetting its existence. "What is what?" Her face had gone stiff with apprehension.

Mokoya could barely think over the blood-rush chorus in her head. "That trinket. Where did you get it?"

The princess licked her lips. "It was a gift. I don't remember who gave it to me." She answered almost immediately, but there was enough of a pause, enough of a note of panic in her voice that Mokoya knew she was lying.

"What's going on?" Thennjay asked.

Mokoya lunged forward. Wanbeng seized her by the wrist, but one pulse through water-nature sent her flying, her hip connecting with an overladen desk. Objects clattered to the ground.

"Nao!" Thennjay exclaimed.

Her hand closed around the anchor. Again: a wash of sensations, a new bouquet of smells and emotions. Orange blossom, sandalwood and incense, a memory of running in the rain and laughing.

Mokoya held it up as Wanbeng scrambled to her feet, wide-eyed. "Where did you get this?" she demanded. "Don't lie to me."

"Give it *back*!" The girl made a swipe for it, clumsy and ineffective.

"Where did you get it?" Mokoya repeated, as Thennjay pleaded in confusion, "Nao . . ."

Wanbeng's feet were broadly planted in a fighting stance, but fear had drained the color from her face. "You don't even know what it is. Why do you care?"

"I know exactly what it is," Mokoya snarled. "Who

gave it to you?" *And why?* she thought. *For what purpose?*

Wanbeng's face turned gemlike, hard and precisely cut. She defiantly tilted her chin upward. "I stole it from Tan Khimyan's room."

Heartbeat like thunder, tropical storm raging in her veins. "Did you?"

"I did. I steal her trinkets all the time. You saw me, and you said *nothing*." Her face flushed. "That thing was hers; now it's mine. Give it back!" The girl made another lunge for it and missed.

Mokoya held the anchor over her head. She was no longer a person, just a collection of screaming nerves. She folded the Slack around herself and was gone.

# Chapter Thirteen

**IT'S NOT AN ANCHOR,** Mokoya thought. *It's a signpost. Or a key to a series of doors.* With the dodecahedron in her hand, the Slack lit up with a constellation of beacons, each one whispering to her with flavors and emotions, a near-overwhelming chorus of feeling.

She picked the one she knew: the tastes of summer, fruit ripe and sweet.

Mokoya unfolded onto the shifting ground outside Bataanar. The sands swallowed her balance and sent her to her knees. She pushed herself upright one-handed, the other still clutched around the anchor. Black fury had swallowed the brilliant shock and confusion on her right arm, turning the skin the color of char, the color of a starless night.

Bramble's serrated form stood stark against the sea of canvas peaks. Phoenix was nestled asleep under her wing, waking as Mokoya strode by, her steps kicking up long plumes of fine sand. Mokoya ignored Phoenix's plaintive bleats as she vanished into the ant-nest interior of the tent city. The incandescence of her anger left little space for anything else.

Rider had lied. They had lied to her, and she had believed them, like a fool. Fuck. Cheebye. Always the trusting one, she never learned, she always ended up regretting it—

Rider was reading, curled on the bed with one of the journals she had given them, when Mokoya entered the tent. The smile on their face evaporated as she stormed toward them. "Mokoya? What—"

Mokoya flung the anchor into their lap. The object rolled off and onto the bed. They stared at it as if it might explode.

"You know what that is, don't you?"

"I—" They twitched like a rabbit.

"Pick it up."

Rider shook their head. "Mokoya, please, let me—"

"*Pick it up.*"

Rider's shaking hands obediently lifted the anchor off the bed. They held it at arm's length. Their voice was reedy: "You went to see the princess."

"You lied to me." The words burst out of Mokoya like spear points through the throat, through the chest. Rage and betrayal were going to split her from the inside, rip her into a thousand shards of flesh and spit her into the wind. "You put this anchor in Tan Khimyan's room. You stole her notes."

They gasped. "What? No. I did not."

"And I wouldn't have known if Wanbeng hadn't taken

the anchor from her room."

Rider pleaded, fingers white against the anchor, "Mokoya, you've got it wrong, I—"

"You summoned that naga."

"No!"

Mokoya struck the anchor from their hands. "Stop *lying* to me!"

Rider cried out and ducked; as Mokoya stood over the bed, chest heaving, dizzy on her feet, she saw that they were curled in an animal cower, pressed to the bed in fear.

The anchor rolled on the ground, grating and grating, its orbits degrading into successively smaller and quicker ones. On the bed Rider shook and gasped. What had she done?

Mokoya's mouth and throat were dry. "I wasn't going to hit you. Rider, I—" She reached out.

Rider flinched. A blink, a shudder in the Slack, and they'd flashed to the other side of the tent. Mokoya turned. "Rider, wait."

"I didn't do it," they whimpered. A groan cracked their voice, like ice the second before it collapsed into rushing river.

Mokoya stepped toward them. "Rider—"

The Slack spasmed. Rider was gone. In their wake they left kaleidoscopic polygons that whispered, *Outside, outside*. Mokoya tried to follow but failed. She wasn't calm or practiced enough for this form of traveling.

She scrambled outside into roiling chaos. In the distance, Bramble bellowed in protest, disturbed from her rest. Rider was leaving.

Mokoya sprinted after them, heels twisting in soft sand. The narrow guts of the tent city were not friendly to quick movement. She collided, shins and elbows and shoulders, with crates and animal cages and irate merchants who spewed obscenities at her. "Cheebye!" she spat back automatically.

She'd seen the kind of fear that now drove Rider. It was the fear of someone who had endured one beating too many.

What had she done?

When she reached Bramble's side, Rider was already mounted. "Wait," she shouted up, "Rider, wait!"

"Don't touch me," Rider beseeched. "Don't come near me."

"I wasn't going to hurt you," Mokoya said. "I would never hit you, I promise."

"I didn't do it," they repeated, as if they had forgotten how to say anything else. They drove their heels into Bramble's side, and the naga took off.

Mokoya collapsed in the tidal wave of displacement. "Rider!" she shouted after them.

Nothing. Bramble cut away into the sky. All strength left Mokoya. The ground was calm, heat and mass and weight, a wide unmoving swath in the Slack. Unlike herself. She wanted to be the ground. She lay down. She stopped moving.

Breath on her neck, a massive nudge against her side and back. Phoenix, agitated, checking in on her. She didn't understand what was happening, why her friend had been taken away, why the one who was not her mother was so upset.

Mokoya wanted to touch Phoenix, wanted to calm this one who was not her daughter. But she couldn't speak or move her head. She floated in and out of focus. Count something. Count your breaths. Say something familiar.

*The Slack is all, and all is the Slack. The Slack is all, and all is the Slack. The Slack is all, and all is the Slack.*

That's how Thennjay found her, lying in the sand, shadowed by Phoenix, mouth moving soundlessly over and over again.

"What's going on, Nao?"

She looked up at him, broad and stark against the sky. His sweat-coated chest heaved with air; he must have run there from the library tower. He was worried. He was right to be worried.

"Rider's gone," she said. "I scared them."

He knelt beside her and helped her up. "Did they do something?"

"They're the ones who called the naga."

Thennjay frowned. "Why would you say that?"

"Because they are." What he needed was an explanation from the old Mokoya, the clever one, the one who wasn't a cracked and draining person.

"That thing you found in Wanbeng's room. That was proof?"

She nodded.

"And you're absolutely sure?"

She inhaled until her chest hurt. She couldn't just nod in assent. She had to say it. Her mind had to form the words, her tongue had to shape them, her lungs had to give them life.

"I am sure," she said.

"Nao, I'm sorry. I don't know what to say." Thennjay held her arms gently. She couldn't tell if it was pity or sympathy in his face. She supposed it didn't matter. "What shall we do now?"

She didn't know. "I need to think."

"Are you going to tell Akeha?"

Something in Thennjay's voice told her he knew that she wasn't sure, that she was lying when she said she was. "Thenn, I need to think. Please, leave me alone for a while." The words came out more desperate than she had intended. "Please."

# Chapter Fourteen

**THE SUN FELL** and rose again while Mokoya dissolved on the bed. She drifted in and out of consciousness, the long, twisted happenings of the day unfurling within her like tea leaves in hot water. Fragmented faces and lines of arguments broke through the surface of her thoughts before sinking again. Things that she had missed or ignored when they happened gained a dubious significance with every successive apparition. In the marsh of half sleep, everything was perfectly logical, but nothing made any sense.

Her capture pearls stood in a line on the makeshift desk, tempting her with their stores of happiness. But they were untouched. Now was not the time.

Eventually a semblance of lucidity returned to her. Outside the tent it was darkening: sunfall again. Had she really lain on the bed for six hours?

Rider loomed heavy in her thoughts. She walked herself through all the brief moments they'd shared together, like a pilgrim circling a sacred arena over and over, hoping to find enlightenment.

Something wasn't right. The map sketched out by the events didn't make sense, didn't join up into a recognizable landscape. Rider was the one controlling the naga, but they were with Mokoya when it attacked the city. Why hadn't Mokoya noticed anything? Why did Rider risk their life fending off the beast?

She regretted lashing out at Rider. In another version of the world, where the threads of fortune had woven a different braid, they could have sat down together and fileted out a sensible truth, exposing the spine of reality that had to be buried within the slippery flesh of lies and narratives.

The bed still smelled faintly of Rider. She was plagued by visions of them as they shivered upon it, as they held up the anchor, terrified of what Mokoya might do. *You went to see the princess,* they had said, their voice quaking.

Mokoya opened her eyes, jolted by realization. Why did Rider say *the princess*? The anchor was supposed to be with Tan Khimyan. Unless—

The last moments in the library tower tore through her head with adrenaline-stripped clarity: the clutter, the blazing light, Wanbeng's nervous flurries of activity.

*Those notes.*

Air occluded Mokoya's chest. Shards of evidence fused into a glittering whole. "She lied to me."

Wanbeng had lied to her. She hadn't stolen the

anchor—it had been in her room all along. Rider had said as much. And it was Wanbeng who had stolen Tan Khimyan's notes. They'd been right there, in her room, hiding in plain sight.

And Rider? Had she colluded with Wanbeng? Or tried to stop her?

She leapt to her feet, scrambling for her talker. She had to tell Thennjay—Akeha—they might all still be in danger—

Too late. A horn wailed from Bataanar's walls.

Cacophony from outside: people shouting. Adi's raptors barking from elsewhere in the camp.

*No.*

Mokoya snatched her cudgel from the ground and ran out of the tent.

There: a sound like a giant's heart beating, the sweep of massive wings. The naga was in the sky, heading straight for the unprotected city, exposed and vulnerable like an oyster cracked open.

Adi and the crew spilled from the tents alongside her. Where was Thennjay? In the city?

Adi grabbed her arm, the wrong one, and the force of her grip sent angry black up the reptile skin. Mokoya pulled it back with a hiss.

"Do something," Adi said.

The naga's mouth opened. It let out a long, peculiar

screech, and fire erupted in a volcanic blossom. The plume scorched the top of Bataanar's outer walls. Mokoya's chest twisted. *Akeha.*

"Watch Phoenix," she told Adi.

The naga sailed over the walls of the city.

Mokoya clenched her fists, held her breath, and folded the Slack.

She stumbled onto uneven rock on the edge of the city and went to her knees. Fifty yields ahead, a man lay burned and dying on the ruined floor, blood seeping through cracked skin. One of Akeha's city guard.

Mokoya reached for water-nature, tensed, leapt forward. The movement carried her fifty yields, a distance no mortal could cover unaided. She landed, tensed, jumped again—from city wall, to roof, to city wall again. The Slack was alive around her, like the wind, singing to her as she sang to it.

She had to get to Wanbeng. She didn't know why the girl was doing this—Some grudge? Punishing her father?—but she had to be stopped.

The naga was circling, coming back for another attack—

*Boom.*

Reds lit the sky. Mokoya fell as the walls shook. Fifty yields away, a cloud of sulfur and carbon billowed into the air. The Machinists had a cannon, a crude solution to the problem of the naga. Crude, but effective: when the creature sailed by overhead, its side was wet with blood.

*Boom.* The Machinists fired again. Smoke and fire cut an arc through the sky from a point on the city wall.

But the naga learned fast. It swerved, terrifyingly quickly for something so massive, raised one wing, and then—

Water-nature pulsed, and the fireball rocketed backward toward its point of origin.

"Cheebye—" Mokoya gasped as she fell forward. The explosion tore into the city wall, the force of it ripping through the stones all along its length.

*Akeha.*

A smoking black crater was gouged into Bataanar where the fireball had landed. She had a searing image of Akeha lying in the rubble, flesh burned raw, bones shattered to pieces, breath failing in scorched and punctured lungs while she scrabbled for something—anything—to tie the threads of him to—

The naga screeched. It was turning toward the center of the city—toward the raja's palace, toward its highest point—

The library tower. The princess.

Mokoya got to her feet. The naga landed on the domed tower in a crouch, its massive wings obscuring half the palace. It dug its hind feet in, tearing into masonry like a child tears through a paper box. Stone rained down in chunks.

Three hundred yields between Mokoya and the library tower. She saw the map of peaked roofs and shingles between them, charted a path, and—

She was off, soaring lighter than air, each leap covering twenty yields, footfalls barely disturbing a scale of roof tile. The naga peeled away from the tower, making another circle, preparing for a second assault. Mokoya saw the hole it had trepanned into the domed roof.

She landed on the dragon-encrusted tip of the raja's receiving pavilion. One more leap and she was at the foot of the library tower, on the ground at last. Stairs wound upward, convoluted and too long to climb. Mokoya jumped from window to window, ignoring the tremor in her limbs, ignoring the deadly quake of her heart. The window in the top layer lay broken open, a yawning lobotomy of cracked roof. She clambered through, tumbled inward, rolled on the floor, and got to her feet.

"Wanbeng," she said, "I know what you're doing. You have to stop."

Among the toppled shelves, the shattered glass, the scattered papers, Wanbeng stood straight as a tree, face incandescent with anger. A traveling box was slung on her back.

"Hello, Tensor," she said scathingly.

The beat of the naga's wings grew louder. The girl seemed unshakably sure of herself, utterly unafraid.

"Why are you doing this?" Mokoya asked.

She sneered. "Haven't you figured it out?"

"No, Wanbeng. Why don't you tell me?"

The girl's face turned sharp and canny. She squatted, gracelessly, and plucked a book from the shambles of the floor. She flung it at Mokoya's chest. "See for yourself."

It was a logbook of some kind, the pages stained with ink, strange dyes. A looping, practiced hand had scrawled observations in thin lines down the pages. There were illustrations, dried samples of things tied in between the sheaves.

The diagrams and results and shorthand were too much to take in, with hell bearing down on them upon ship-sail wings.

"Wanbeng, what is this?"

Wanbeng looked triumphant. "They thought they could *lie* to me. Keep me from the capital when Mother was dying and hide the truth. They were wrong. I'm not a child any longer. I'm not an *idiot*."

Her words weren't registering. Mokoya could see the naga now, the fire in its eyes. So close its flight tore howling wind into the ruined chamber. "What are you saying?"

Wanbeng's eyes glittered. "Don't you see, Tensor? That's my *mother*."

*No*, Mokoya wanted to say. It was unthinkable.

Yet the pieces were all there: The naga was an adept. The Tensors had to have found a soul pattern from somewhere. And hadn't Tan Khimyan and Raja Choonghey become close, in the capital, when Raja Ponchak fell ill?

The naga hit the tower again. Everything shuddered. A chunk of wall came away like steamed cake in the hands of a greedy child. A head, massive and serrated, reared into the chamber, bringing with it a wash of heat, of musk. Wanbeng ran toward it.

"Wanbeng, no!" Mokoya started after her.

The naga lowered its head, and before Mokoya could react or deflect the blow, she was hit in the stomach by a raw fist of air. The ground met her spine, hard.

Pain screamed from her knee to her hip as she scrambled to her feet. Wanbeng had climbed onto the naga's massive head and was sliding down its neck, looking for a place to rest. "Wanbeng—listen to me—"

The naga beat its wings, trying to drive Mokoya off her feet again. She gritted her teeth and pushed back against it, preparing to fold the Slack. She'd be gravesent if she let the girl run off with this wild creature.

Opening her mindeye this close to the naga, she finally noticed the unnatural alterations that had been done to it, the thing grafted to its soul.

Mokoya's fold carried her onto one of the naga's hind

legs as it took off into the sky. Its skin was hot and rough, and it stank with the musk of a hundred horses. Her feet held against its leathery texture. She climbed upward.

"Get lost," Wanbeng shouted from the top of the naga. "You can't change my mind!"

Was this what it was like, being on a boat at sea? One foot slipped, and Mokoya barely caught herself in time. Below she could see the glint of water reflecting flame and moonlight. Wind tore at her as the naga flew onward, away from the city.

"Leave me and my mother alone," the girl cried.

"It's not your mother," Mokoya said, over the howl of wind and sand. "This isn't—" She sucked in a breath. "Look at it! It's a beast, a wild animal."

"You're *wrong.*"

In her words, Mokoya heard the echoes of her arguments with Thennjay about Phoenix. "I'm *not.*" She kept climbing. "Trust me, Wanbeng. I know what you're feeling. I know what it's like."

The girl understood her meaning, but she wasn't swayed. She shouted, her breaths harsh, "Just because *you've* given up on your daughter, doesn't mean you're right!"

"Your mother is gone," Mokoya shouted back. "You have to accept that."

Wanbeng's features crumpled in rage. "You stay away

from me!" And she struck outward with earth-nature, hitting Mokoya in the chest.

She stumbled. The naga pitched, and Mokoya lost her grip on its skin. Something struck her head hard. The world exploded in flashes of black as she felt herself in free fall, the shape of the naga receding, Wanbeng's cry of "Tensor Sanao?" pulling away to silence. The cold embrace of water slapped around her, and darkness took her as the oasis folded over her head.

ACT THREE

# THE RED THREADS
# OF FORTUNE

# Chapter Fifteen

**MOKOYA WAS FALLING, SLIDING**, running up a rocky slope, red dirt in her eyes, her fingernails, her mouth. Her chest hurt like a shot wound, but there was no blood, just panic.

She knew what was happening. She knew, and she couldn't stop it.

Her desperate knees and feet found the top of the slope, found the great plateau of the battle, found the source of the death smell. Blood. Guts. Burnt hide. The naga, stricken: mouth open, sides heaving, hole torn so deep its white ribs gleamed. And Rider, crumpled there: eyes half open, neck broken-angled, blood tracing calligraphy on their face.

"Rider!" Mokoya scooped them up, pulled them in, shook their senseless form. Found them heavy, inert, limbs dangling, skull dragging against rock. Slackcraft flared across their skin, tattoos stirring awake, burning through dead flesh and onto bone.

Mokoya folded in half and screamed.

Thennjay said, "I'm sorry, Nao. You know you couldn't

have changed anything." There was blood on his robes, a weapon in his hand, a sorrowful expression on his face.

Had they been in battle? Why was he here? Why was *she* here?

Someone called her name. Like an herb bag being pulled out of soup, everything rushed away from her.

She woke to pressure on her back and hips, a sour taste in her mouth, and a symphony of pains and aches she could not begin to catalogue. Shock and fear forced her body upright anyway. She knew this place, this quiet cavern, with its light and warmth and sounds of soft water.

"Mokoya." Rider appeared in her field of vision, an almost-blur of gray and cream. A jolt to her being—Rider was here, alive and unbroken. They were trying to keep Mokoya down on the soft fabric that made up a bed.

Mokoya pushed their hands away, struggling to get to her feet—to do what? She got halfway up, then sat back down. Her clothes had a stiffness to them that told her they'd recently dried out. How was she still in one piece? She should have shattered. She should have died.

Rider looked exhausted, their face bloodless and fragile as cracked porcelain. "Mokoya," they whispered. "Thank the heavens."

Behind Rider, Bramble was curled on the ground with her wings folded in, observing them. Bataanar and its destruction felt very distant. "What happened?" she asked.

They reached a hand toward Mokoya's face, reconsidered, withdrew. "Where should I begin?"

"Wherever you can. Just tell me what happened." She kept her voice gentle. She did not scream, although she wanted to.

Rider pulled at the joints of their fingers and wrists repeatedly. "I had time to think. I regretted what happened between us. So I came back to Bataanar. I did not expect the attack. It took me by surprise." They bit their lip, looked away.

"You saw the attack. What then?"

"I saw the attack. I saw you fall into the water. We saved you, but you would not wake. I brought you back here."

"How long has it been?"

"One sun-cycle."

"That's too long." The city was in ruins, the princess in the wilds with that beast. Alarm pushed Mokoya to her feet against the protests of her body. A wave of dizziness overtook her. She staggered, and Rider's arms were there, holding her up. Mokoya sagged. She felt like she had been running up cliff faces for hours.

They were almost cheek and cheek. Rider's face brimmed with emotion, and all Mokoya could see was that same face, ashen and blood-glazed. She looked at the ring of characters circling their neck and remembered them flaring to life, branding themselves upon ribs and vertebrae as Rider slipped irretrievably away from her.

She'd had a prophecy for the first time in four years. She didn't understand why the visions had chosen to come back to her *now*. But one thing was certain.

Sometime in the near future, Rider was going to die.

She let Rider guide her back down onto the bed. She cupped a hand against their cheek as they tried to draw away. Rider blinked. "Mokoya?"

She inscribed circles on their cheekbone with her thumb, haunted by the butcher-fresh memory of their viscera heavy in her arms, their chest cold and still. Words choked her throat like weeds.

Rider pressed their forehead against hers. All the fear Mokoya had seen earlier was gone, replaced by guilt. Their skin was damp, radiating heat.

"It was the princess behind it all," Mokoya said.

"Yes."

"And you knew."

"Yes." A shiver ran through their body. "I hid it from you, Mokoya. That was my decision."

"Why?"

They sat back on their heels, drawing themselves out of her grasp. "Mokoya," they said, the syllables a heavy sigh. "I did not trust you. We had only just met. I could not be certain what you would do if I told you the truth.

And I still believed that the princess could be reasoned with. I believed I could overcome her stubbornness."

"But you were wrong," she said quietly.

"I was, on both accounts. When I saw the ruins of the city, when I saw you plunge into the oasis, I thought, *I've killed her. If I had just told her, I would not have—*" Their voice grew small. *"I would not have lost her."*

"Don't blame yourself," Mokoya said. "We've all been fools here." There had been no greater conspiracy at work, no nefarious plot to destroy cities or bring down empires. Just a heartbroken young woman who missed her mother.

She reached forward and grasped Rider's hand in hers. Rider looked down at the jade tones of her pebbled skin. "Green is for sadness," they said softly.

"You remembered."

"It is my fault."

"No." Mokoya withdrew her hand. "Not exactly."

Rider studied her intently. "You had a vision before you woke."

"Yes. A prophecy." Mokoya hesitated, then reached for her belt and withdrew the still-warm pearl from her capture box. She could feel the vision trapped in it, the thick sourness of death solid in her palm.

Caution had entered Rider's voice. "What did you see?"

Mokoya weighed the blood-soaked future in her hand, pressing her lips together. Unable to put words to any of that horror, she held the pearl out to Rider.

They took it. Brightness and color blossomed in the Slack as they read what was stored within. Their eyes went wide as they watched the vision replay. Then their brows creased. "I see," they said softly.

Rider got up, turning away from Mokoya, still holding the pearl. They paced wordlessly with the sluggish movements of one walking through a storm.

Mokoya got to her feet, much more slowly this time. The dizziness came again, but she let the star-tainted wave of it wash over her and remained standing. "Rider? Are you all right?"

Rider gazed at the break in the roof of the cavern, where the sky revealed itself in brilliant tones and the cascade of the oasis sang and caught the sun, unperturbed by the troubles of humankind. Finally they turned to Mokoya, haloed by daylight, face made invisible by the glare. "So be it," they said. "If that is to be my fate, then I embrace it."

Rider sounded glad, which frightened her. Mokoya crossed the space between them. "Rider, I don't—"

"No." Rider put a hand to her lips. "It is a good thing. It means we kill the creature. The city can be saved."

"A good thing?" Mokoya managed.

"A good thing," Rider repeated, softly. Mokoya leaned forward, collapsing the weight of her head on Rider's, her breaths coming in sharp and painful spurts. They placed their hands, palms flat, against Mokoya's damp cheeks. "You survive. You carry on. Someone who will remember me the way I want to be remembered. It's a good thing."

"Rider—" Mokoya's shoulders shook. She wanted to tear Rider out of the Slack, rip them from the threads of fate they had been woven into. She felt entombed by the cruelty of the fortunes, trapped in an endless, formless darkness.

"We must return to the city," Rider said. Their voice was calm, the melancholy in it stripped away. "There is much left to do."

# Chapter Sixteen

THENNJAY AND AKEHA MET them in front of the city. Bataanar, remarkably, still appeared whole, and the tent city had the same chaotic energy as fabric being woven. Busy figures, cloth-wrapped to the point of anonymity, cleared away debris. Chatter filled the background, indistinct and constant like the sea upon the shore.

"We thought you were dead," Thennjay said, after she slid from Bramble's back onto the sand. His skin had a pale, ashen aspect to it, like a layer of dust had settled permanently on him. She knew she was just imagining it.

Akeha said nothing. He simply enveloped Mokoya in a rib-grinding hug and held her there until the tremble in his breathing dissipated. Mokoya wasn't sure how she could comfort him. She couldn't bring herself to say the words "I'm all right, I'm alive." Both parts of that sentence felt like a lie. She was a ghost, her feet not really touching the ground.

When he let her go, she said, "We must speak with the raja."

Akeha started to laugh, a sound dry as bones rattling

in an urn, a small hint of mania bubbling underneath. She hoped he wasn't breaking as she had broken. "The raja's busy. He has an *interrogation* to conduct. But come. Let's provide him some company."

~

They had imprisoned Tan Khimyan in the rock under Bataanar. The jail was windowless, artificially lit, smooth- and dark-walled. Iron latticework stood between the prisoner and the raja, and a damper hummed in her half of the cell. The device pulled distractingly and disruptively on the Slack in irregular cycles. No slackcrafting their way out of this room. Mokoya felt herself unraveling in its lull.

"This is gross injustice," Tan Khimyan said. She had a paleness that spoke of injury, not delicacy, and her hair and clothes were in disarray. "After all I have done for your family—"

"*For* my family?" Raja Choonghey's voice was a blade, cutting through the slow chill of the cell. "You *destroyed* my family."

Beside Mokoya, Rider had gone tense at the sight of their former lover. She reached for their clenched fist and worked her fingers into it, although she wasn't sure who was comforting whom.

Raja Choonghey was thinner than in the pictures and looked older than Mokoya had expected. Shadows carved relief into the landscape of his face; his brow was bisected by a valley of old worries, and his mouth was framed by a deep furrow on either side. His hair, at fifty, was milk-white.

"You told me Ponchak died. You said you couldn't save her." He hurled something in her direction: a book, which struck the iron grille and thumped to the floor spine first, falling open at her feet. Mokoya recognized the logbook Wanbeng had thrown at her, battered from its ordeal in the library tower. "You turned her into this *creature.*"

"Ponchak *volunteered* for the experiment," Tan Khimyan said. "She was obsessed with immortality. You may deny it as much as you like, but you know it to be true."

"And yet you did nothing!"

"I argued against this atrocity! But my colleagues would not listen. They wanted a Tensor soul."

"And did you stop them? No! You are just as guilty as they are. I should have your head, you worthless snake."

Rider interrupted their exchange. "Executing her will not solve our problems."

The raja turned, frowning at the one who dared to speak without being spoken to. For the first time, he seemed to notice the presence of others in the room. "Who are you?"

"I am Rider. We have met, although I think you do not remember."

The raja studied Rider like a dead animal he was trying to identify. Slow, disdainful recognition spread. "No, no. I do remember you. You were this woman's pet, weren't you?" He hacked out a laugh. "Yes, you were her little amusement. No wonder you keep such contemptible company now. Like that one." He looked at Akeha, a sneer distorting his face.

"Of course expecting gratitude from you would be too much," Akeha said. "We merely saved your city from destruction."

"Your Greatness," Thennjay said, "little will be achieved by our quarreling. Your daughter's safety should be our main concern."

"Oh? Are you saying it isn't my main concern?" Raja Choonghey had a voice like vinegar: colorless, but with the ability to eat through metal. "You should be more careful with your words, Venerable One."

Thennjay bowed in apology. "I apologize for my rudeness."

"We can help you," Mokoya said. "We know where to find Wanbeng."

A brief shudder went through the raja, and that quake

unearthed a glimpse of an exhausted, grieving father, a man Mokoya could empathize with. Then suspicion clouded his features. "And how would you know that?"

"I saw it in a prophecy," she said quietly.

A hush smothered the room. Fear flickered in the raja's expression. "What did you see? Did you see her? Was Wanbeng hurt?"

"I—" Mokoya exhaled. "I don't know. You should look for yourself." The room's chill glacial creep was claiming her bones, and the damper's droning song hurt her head. "But not here."

Pride held the raja's stone-edged demeanor in place as he surveyed them. His mouth twisted, very slightly, as he met Akeha's defiant gaze. "Very well," he finally said. He instructed the guard at the door to "watch that snake in her box," and left the room without looking back.

As they followed in his wake, Tan Khimyan called out, "Swallow!"

Rider hesitated, took a faltering half step forward, then turned to face their former lover. They said nothing; there was no need. Their face was a graven message.

"This turn of events must please you," she said.

"Nothing about this sequence of events pleases me," Rider said.

"But you have what you want now, do you not?" She spread her hands, indicating her imprisonment.

"Again, you understand nothing of what I want."

"Don't I? I was a victim of your scheme. Now you have moved on. You've found a bigger, juicier fish to suck dry." She laughed. "One no less than the Protector's own daught—"

Mokoya's hand snapped up into a fist. Water-nature tightened around Tan Khimyan's neck. Her words cut off, and her face contorted, hands scrabbling for air. The damper in the cell was no match for Mokoya's rage, tar-black and potent.

"Mokoya," Rider gasped.

"If the raja decides to execute you, I will encourage him," she hissed at the imprisoned woman.

Tan Khimyan's face purpled like fruit ripening. Rider threw themselves around Mokoya, their trembling arms latching in the small of her back. "Mokoya. Please, stop."

They only detached themselves when Mokoya let go of Tan Khimyan's trachea. Akeha was laughing. "Well *done*, Moko. I've wanted to do that for *years*."

Thennjay cleared his throat. "We should not keep the raja waiting," he said. "Come."

# Chapter Seventeen

IT WAS STRANGE, Mokoya thought, watching a prophecy from outside her head.

In the raja's receiving chambers, cracked and disheveled from the naga's attack, Rider generated their geometrical tessellations that both bypassed and encompassed all five natures of the Slack. The capture pearl in their hands pierced the air with strange light. Above the table they had gathered around, the prophecy came to life in a blur of moving images and distorted sound.

The events still lingered in her head: half memory, half nightmare. For a moment, watching her other self grieve over Rider's body, Mokoya had a sense that she was not real. That she was not a person, but merely a mirage invented by the fortunes. She shivered. Around the table a bouquet of emotions played out on faces: shock on the raja's, sorrow on Thennjay's, anger on Akeha's. Rider's expression was impenetrable.

The prophecy ended as she remembered, leaving unnerved silence in its wake. Rider allowed the audience to absorb what they had just seen.

Thennjay met Mokoya's gaze, his eyes sad. She looked away. The feeling that she existed on a different plane of the world from everyone else had stayed with her.

"This gives us enough landmarks to locate the naga," Rider said.

The raja wet his lips. "Was that real?" he asked, gesturing at the air where the prophecy had been.

Akeha tilted his head. "Are you questioning a prophet's vision?"

He swallowed. The scene—blood, death, grief—had clearly shaken him. "Then you will die," he said to Rider.

"Indeed. It is a fate I have accepted."

Raja Choonghey moved away from the table and paced impatiently. The pop of his knuckles as he cracked them was the only sound in the room. His frown burrowed more deeply into his face. "But the vision did not show my daughter's fate."

"No," Rider said. "And that is good. She should not be there. In my plan we would take her to safety before I deal with the naga." They pointed. "Mokoya will do it. She has learned skills that allow her to travel instantaneously."

Mokoya's cheeks burned at this tiny betrayal, at Rider roping her into their suicide mission without her consent, but she said nothing.

Raja Choonghey rubbed his face. "This is madness," he said. "I can't risk my daughter's life on these illusions."

"These illusions are proven," Rider said.

"Do you have a better plan?" Akeha added.

The raja struck him with a glare, jawbone milling through his anger. Finally he said to Rider, "Very well. If that is your choice, then that is what we shall do."

~

As they were leaving the chamber, Thennjay caught Mokoya by the arm to draw her aside. "Nao . . ." he said. His expression did the rest of the talking for him.

"Don't worry about me," she replied, flat and practiced, like she was reading off the lines of the First Sutra.

He rubbed the skin of her lizard arm, where the colors had faded to a muddy blue-gray. "I can't help it."

Mokoya wanted to say, *It's all right, I'm all right, everything is going to be all right.* But faking a smile required energy; steadying her voice required strength. And she felt emptied of both.

So she said, "I'm tired," and leaned into his bulk. Thennjay wrapped his warm, solid arms around her. Mokoya imagined herself dissolving in his embrace, her molecules scattering unconscious and pain-free to the ends of the known world.

All her life she had been stalked by a particular shadow of fear. In its teeth this specter held visions in which her loved ones were hurt and killed. She would lie awake at night, feeling the prickle of a prophecy creeping toward her, and be terrified of falling asleep, just in case she woke to a vision of Thennjay succumbing to poison, or Akeha lying in a back alley with a blade through his heart.

When the accident killed her daughter, she had been furious at the shadow for betraying her, for not showing her an actual tragedy when it was about to happen. She had wanted to know, or thought she had wanted to know. Sometimes she thought this anger was what had driven her prophetic ability away.

Now it had returned after many years, and it had brought her this gift as though mocking her. She had been wrong. She did not want to know. It was not making the pain any easier.

Thennjay held her until she somehow found the will to separate from him. "Go to them," he said softly. "You still have time."

~

Rider had fled to the tent city, as though they could not stand to be in Bataanar a moment longer than necessary. When Mokoya found them, they were crouched by Bramble, stroking the naga's snout as they whispered in a language Mokoya did not know. She stood watching them, afraid of shattering this moment of languid tenderness.

Rider looked up. "Mokoya."

She approached them slowly, her limbs heavy as though she dragged a promise of violence in her wake. Rider looked at her, patient, waiting for her to speak.

"She was the one who hit you," Mokoya finally said. "Tan Khimyan."

"It's past," Rider said. "It does not matter."

"The past always matters," Mokoya said. Especially when there was no future to hold on to.

Rider nodded slowly. "She often got into bad moods. And it would be my fault, for behaving so badly, for provoking her temper. She would say those things to me."

"You weren't to blame. Violence is the fault of the one enacting it. Always."

"I know that, Mokoya. I know now."

She touched their face gently, trailed fingers down their chin and the tendons of their neck, ending at the border of words spelling Rider's life story. "Why didn't you just leave, then?" Not an accusation, but curiosity. She wanted to understand Rider.

"Because I loved her, Mokoya. Because I was a fool back then, terrified by a city and a world I did not understand." They hesitated. "And because of my daughter."

Mokoya froze. "Your daughter?"

Rider broke away to search through one of Bramble's saddlebags. They returned with a picture scroll, which they unrolled and tensed to life. The thin brown sheet lit up with a looping, repeating sliver of life: an olive-skinned young woman, generously dimpled, laughing in the sunlight.

"This is Echo," Rider said. "She was an orphan I met on streets of Chengbee years ago. All the time we lived in the capital, Khimyan never suspected I was helping raise a girl in a workshop in the Lower Quarter."

The girl had such a lightness to her smile, a radiant glow of hope. "Where is she now?"

"She lives in Chengbee still. She is grown now, a dragonboat jouster and an apprentice to a medicine seller." They pressed the scroll into Mokoya's hands. "When this is over, will you look for her? For my sake?"

She cradled the scroll between her fingers. "What should I tell her?"

"Tell her I died protecting those I care for. She will understand."

Who was Rider protecting, and from what? Mokoya nodded anyway. "What else will you have me do?"

"I would ask you to watch Bramble." Behind them, the naga rumbled at mention of her name. "She will stay behind when we execute the plan. Since she did not feature in your prophecy, her fate is not yet locked. I would like her to survive."

Mokoya frowned at their phrasing, *her fate is not yet locked.* It struck her as strange, for reasons she could not identify. Rider continued, "Bramble has never lived without human companionship. She would not survive in the wild."

"Phoenix won't object to a playmate," she allowed. "Anything else?"

"My bones." As Mokoya sucked in a breath, they said, "They will be a record of who I am . . . who I was. I would like you to keep them. Your husband could perform the death rituals, could he not?"

She wanted to say, *You were supposed to teach me how to read the words,* but what would be the point of saying that, except to cause them more grief?

"We could preserve the bones, yes," she said. "Is that all?"

"There is one more thing."

"Tell me, then."

"I want you to live."

Air thickened in Mokoya's lungs. "What?"

Rider's hands wrapped gently around her arms as though she were an eggshell carving, fragile and precious. "I want you to embrace what fortune has bestowed upon you. I want you to look ahead with no regrets. I want you to carry the memory of what happened here into the future."

Mokoya could not tamp down her reaction. "I can't do that. I can't pretend that it's all okay—"

Rider sighed. "You blame yourself for this."

"I know it's foolish. I know I don't shape the prophecies. I know things happen that I cannot change, but—"

They put a thin finger to her lips. "Hush. In another iteration of the world, we might never have met. It was fortune's blessing that we did."

"In another iteration of the world, you would live on."

"Yet this is the one we have been given. We must make the best of it we can."

Mokoya pressed her forehead to theirs and gasped her way through the torrent of emotions engulfing her. Their trembling fingers clung to the bones of her cheek and neck.

Rider's breath ghosted over her lips. "Lie with me," they whispered, brimming with heat. "Forget the world in my embrace. While we still can."

"Yes." She would have let Rider swallow her alive if they'd asked. There was nothing she would deny them. Not now.

# Chapter Eighteen

**MOKOYA STRUGGLED TO FIND** sleep. Unease chewed at the corners of her consciousness, as though she had forgotten something, but could not remember what. Next to her Rider, exhausted and fragrant, had fallen into a pattern of deep and easy breaths. They'd spent hours describing life in the Quarterlands, telling of thousand-yield trees that took days to climb, of ringed dwellings that nestled in the canopies, of forest floors dark and unfathomable as the bottom of the ocean.

Mokoya had listened, their hands clasped between her own, trying to press every aspect of the scene into indelible memory. She had one advantage, Rider had said: this time, she already knew what the pattern of grief felt like. She would be prepared for what was to come.

Mokoya watched them sleep and tried to feel tenderness, but the unease was overwhelming, like a cramp in her fingers and toes. It drove her up, onto her feet, and out of the tent.

The sky was still dark. They had planned to set out perhaps an hour before next sunrise: the pugilists, the crew, a few of the Machinists. And Rider, of course.

Mokoya walked the tangled, sleeping intestines of the tent city until she came to its edge, where Bramble and Phoenix nested, quiet and unburdened. The oasis lapped gently at its borders. Mokoya rose onto the balls of her feet, five times, ten. It did not help.

She paced several circles into the sand and then sat cross-legged in the middle of that track. She cleared her mind, blanked her mindeye, and tried to calm her uneasiness with the weight of the Slack.

*The Slack is all, and all is the Slack.*

Her recitation failed. Mokoya had always been a poor student of meditation, and her mind worked against her now, scraping against her skull. Everything she heard and felt was a distraction: blood surging in her veins, wind singing, oasis moistening the night air, the hot breaths of Phoenix and Bramble nearby.

Memories, images, impressions spiraled. Rider's voice surfaced, saying, *Since she did not feature in your prophecy, her fate is not yet locked.*

*Her fate is not yet locked.* As if her visions caused the future, and not the other way around.

Why had Rider asked her if she folded the Slack to make her visions, as if she had control over the passage of time, over the twists and braids of fortune?

Mokoya reached for that folding trick again, trying to

look at the Slack in a different way. She thought of the way Rider's slackcrafting *felt*, intricate patterns generated from movement behind the curtains of what she knew. The Slack was not just divided into five natures—that was the Tensorate way of thinking—but infinitely malleable, not a layer over the world but an integral part of it, inseparable from the objects it governed, more all-encompassing than the First Sutra could have ever expressed.

She dissolved all her thoughts, dissolved her mind-eye.

Yet it wasn't enough. She had to do more than that.

Dissolve the trappings of Monastery training. Discard the frameworks of Tensor study.

Dissolve memory, dissolve personhood. She was no longer Mokoya, yet she remained unchanged. A collection of occurrences in space and time, mathematical possibilities intersecting and colliding, not a living thing but a coalescence of probabilities.

And then, as though lightning-struck, the thing that was once Sanao Mokoya saw it. That thing faced the Slack as the Quarterlanders must, raw and contiguous and endless.

The Slack is all, and all is the Slack.

Time and space were just another aspect of the Slack, this fabric of the universe they were woven into. They faded in and out of focus. Sometimes they were like sheets of rice paper upon which everything marched. Sometimes they were embedded into the soup in which everything swam, just another ingredient, no more divisible than salt was from spiced broth. Sometimes they were both.

The way this thing called Sanao Mokoya was connected to the Slack was different from the way the others were connected, sleeping in their tents or stacked within Bataanar's walls. The time nature of the Slack coiled around them, called to them, separate from what they called the five natures, separate from everything else. Yet all the same. Indivisible. Colors upon colors all melding into one color.

You couldn't understand it if you looked only for the five natures. But once it came to you, there was no way of unseeing it.

A prophet could control the time-nature of the Slack. Those visions, born from her unconscious mind, were her uncontrolled attempts to rearrange the patterns in the Slack. And once they were laid down, those patterns became locked to the prophet's destiny. The thing that was Mokoya saw Rider's death, bound to her against the patterns of the Slack by threads of fortune.

For a prophecy to be undone, the prophet herself had to be undone.

Mokoya opened her eyes. She was lying on hot sand, limbs trembling with the force of enlightenment, heart pumping with the shock of understanding. She sat up, feeling like an entirely new being, resting with her hip-bones against the hungry floor of the desert, at once detached from and yet one with the universe around her. The Slack sang to her, songs she had never heard before, its threads ringing like zither strings.

Prophecies *could* be undone. They had just gone about it the wrong way.

Mokoya got to her feet and was amazed when they held beneath her. They led her back to her tent. She knew what she had to do.

Rider still lay asleep on their cot. Mokoya had no intention of waking them. She crouched on one knee to get a clearer look at their face. Peaceful, unbothered.

"You knew," she said softly. "You've always known. But you didn't tell me, because you wanted to protect me. You knew what I would do. I understand. I forgive you."

Rider did not stir. The day's happenings had truly exhausted them. Mokoya stood, quiet as the breath of trees. She had letters to write.

～

JY Yang

*Dearest Rider,*

*I hope you can forgive me.*

*Do not be alarmed. I have gone to face the naga by myself; that is my choice. I have discovered the truth that you, I think, were trying to save me from. I saw in the Slack how to undo the knots of the prophecy that I created. I saw that it was possible to save you.*

*Even if it costs my life, I have decided to do it. More than anything, I want you to live.*

*Do not feel sorry for me. I am not angry, nor am I sad. This has come as a relief to me. In fact, I feel joy.*

*Since the days of my childhood, when these prophecies started to plague me, I have struggled with helplessness. Oftentimes I felt trapped at the bottom of a frozen pond, watching things happen through the ice, unable to touch them, unable to change anything. I felt nothing but hatred: toward myself, toward my visions, toward the world. It was as if fortune itself were mocking me.*

*After my daughter died, I decided the only way to avoid more pain was to leave. I knew I was running away when I left the capital, but I cared little. I kept running. If I wasn't around anyone, if I didn't care about anything, then there could be no hurt, and no one to hurt.*

*Living like that, it would have been a matter of time before things came to their logical conclusion. So do not feel regret for my sake. By ending this way, at least something positive will be gained from my death.*

*I wish we could have met under better circumstances. Perhaps in a time to come, in another world (as you said), we will. To have known you, even for one day, was a gift to me, fortune's penance. I have only one wish for you:*

*Live on, dear one. Embrace what fortune has bestowed upon you. Look ahead with no regrets. And carry a memory of me into the future.*


*Mokoya*

# Chapter Nineteen

**SHE TOOK NOTHING WITH** HER, as one does when one does not intend to return. Her cudgel she left in the tent; she would not need it against her foe.

She would serve as a distraction, a focal point for the naga's slackcraft, to give Wanbeng time to get to safety. She would surprise the creature, break its neck with earth-nature to limit the damage it could do.

If she could, she would kill it. Either way, she did not expect to survive.

She was ready.

Outside her tent, Mokoya closed her eyes against the lightening sky and folded the Slack.

The naga had nested in open air on the far side of the oasis, where water cascaded down massive boulders to a reflecting pool below. A raised plateau about two hundred yields across stood between the oasis and the sunken pool. That was where Mokoya came out of the fold, tumbling over her own feet and into a roll, dry dust filling her mouth. Her head struck something lumpy, and sand-noise dizziness flared as she stood. She was right in front of the naga's massive bulk, radiating animal stink.

The creature struggled to its feet, nostrils flaring, a growl building in its throat.

So much for surprising it.

"Who goes there?" demanded a voice.

Wanbeng was alive, imperious as ever, standing between the creature's winged front limbs.

"Wanbeng! It's me."

"Tensor Sanao?" The girl's eyes widened.

The naga bared its teeth and lunged its head forward. "No!" the girl commanded.

Her hand snapped up as she tensed through forest-nature. The naga froze, then backed down.

The creature's breathing was labored. Blood oozed from its sides and marked wide smears on the ground. The Machinists' fire cannon had struck deep. The naga was dying, its wounds slowly draining its blood, the great rot setting in.

Mokoya said to the girl: "It's me, Wanbeng. I've come to help."

"You're not dead."

"Not yet."

"Then I'm not a criminal." Her voice shook with relief.

Unreasonable hope seized Mokoya: What if this ordeal was survivable? "Wanbeng, we must end this creature's misery," she said. "Look at its wounds."

"Those *murderers* did this."

"You saw what it did to the city. You know it's dangerous."

The girl couldn't answer the accusations. She didn't argue with Mokoya, did not insist on the naga's humanity. The delusion had been wrung from her in the hours since. In a way, Mokoya almost envied her. Wanbeng's eyes shone with bright frustration, the lines around them evidence of her exhaustion. "I don't want to go back. I don't want to be my father's little *puppet*."

"You don't have to be. Wanbeng, I promise I will do all I can to help you. But there's nothing out here. I know, because I've spent the last two years of my life hiding in the wilderness. It won't help."

The girl bit her lip. "What are you going to do?"

"I'm—" Mokoya exhaled. "I'm going to undo what has been done," she said. "I'm going to untangle the soulgraft."

"What do you want me to do?"

"Keep it still while I work the slackcraft. Can you do that?"

Wanbeng's shoulders moved. "I'll try."

Mokoya calmed her mindeye and read the creature in front of her. She could see what had been done to the essence of the wild naga. Raja Ponchak's soul pattern had been grafted on, precisely and artificially, a profusion of

Slack-connections fastened to the naga at five points, like a pentagonal tumor. The naga's body had grown to enormous proportions in response to the injury that had been done to its soul, accumulating matter and complexity to balance this unasked-for addition.

The deed had been done with calculated artlessness. She despised the ones responsible.

She had to work fast: she didn't know how long Wanbeng could keep the naga still once she started. She began to unravel the first knot, dissolving the connections that held it together.

The Slack *resisted.* The prophecy tangled around her pulled back against her efforts, choking her slackcraft. Refusing to let her unfix what had been fixed.

Mokoya, existing half outside her own head, saw a path through the snarl. She twisted the Slack. Bright connections sprang free. The first knot disintegrated.

The naga screeched and tried to rear up on its hind legs. "No! *Don't!*" Wanbeng pulled through forest-nature, holding the naga back. The creature's anger and pain disrupted slackcraft, rippling in waves, making everything more difficult.

Mokoya reached for the second knot and twisted the fabric of the world. The knot came undone to another cry of pain, another seismic spasm through the Slack. The third slipped from her as the naga bucked, trying to break from Wanbeng's control—

"Tensor, hurry!" The girl's voice was strained. "I can't hold on—"

Mokoya undid the third knot. The naga bellowed and swept one wing forward. Wanbeng shrieked as she was knocked backward.

"No!" Mokoya made a mad tense for the fourth knot and missed. The naga swung one wing at her, and she tensed a layer of solid air between them, the naga bouncing off it with a sound of rage.

"Wanbeng, run!" Mokoya gasped, a moment before the naga struck her with a ball of raw force, water-nature. She flew backward. Her arm made an ugly sound as she landed, and instinct drove her into a roll. Jaws descended, and Mokoya narrowly escaped their massive snap.

She tensed through earth-nature, pulling the naga's head to the ground and keeping it there.

In her mindeye she saw probabilities converging upon her, driven by her manipulation of the Slack. She knew what was coming. She welcomed it.

"Tensor!" Wanbeng was still alive, thank the fortunes. She felt the girl's effort in the Slack, trying to wrest back control of the situation, and felt a spark of admiration.

Mokoya pulled at the fourth knot as the naga clawed at the Slack, but its soul was so ragged the motion came out glancing and crooked. A spasm through water-energy, meant to bury her in a wave of lifted sand, only flung her backward. Something in her hip tore as she landed, and she cried out.

The fourth knot, frayed by the naga's frantic attempts to tense, had come undone. The soul-graft was loose in the Slack, anchored only on one point. It was unraveling and flailing in all directions, pulling at the soul essence of the naga, tearing it. The Slack warped with the unnatural energy, and the naga arched over her in both physical and metaphysical pain.

The naga knew who was causing it all that pain.

Mokoya braced herself as the naga snatched her up with one clawed hand. She felt gravity lurch as she shot skyward, her lower body crushed under massive pressure. Pain consumed her, and black spots burst through her vision.

There was only one thing on her mind. Mokoya pulled at the last knot as hard as she could. There was no time for focus or delicacy: just a pure surge of energy into the fabric of the Slack.

The fifth knot broke. The graft tore away, unraveling into nothingness.

The naga screamed. There was motion, an impression of being flung into the air, gravity calling, speed, a blur of dark and light. Something that looked like the sky whirled over Mokoya, and then her body struck ground, broken and crunching, a sack with a ripped seam spilling its warm contents onto sand.

The sun was rising, and she wasn't really in her body anymore. The thing that was Sanao Mokoya dwindled to a string of thoughts as her consciousness faded.

*There. I did it. I changed what couldn't be changed. I've cut the red threads of fortune.*

*Now I am free.*

# Chapter Twenty

SUNLIGHT AND BREEZE GREETED the cemetery like old friends, daubing the koi pond with light and the hillside with the pattern of leaves. The gentle fingers of willow trees swayed in the wind, brushing their tips against the gravestones in the Sanao family quarter. The ground exhaled the scent of yesterday's rain as Rider knelt before the newest stone in the quarter, the red paint on the granite still vivid. From a distance came the faint hubbub of life, the chatter of voices from inns and the old songs of cowherds.

Rider tensed a small flame and lit a stick of incense. Smoke unraveled from its tip, redolent with sandalwood and ash.

As Rider stood, Mokoya took their hand. "Thank you for coming with me today." She swept a glance over her daughter's grave, bright and blissful, and felt her belly grow warm. "I wish you could have met her somehow."

Rider squeezed her fingers. "Your memories of her are enough."

Screams and laughter intruded upon their peace: the

twins, playing a game of catch-the-thief. Rider colored. "Children! This is a graveyard, not a playground. Show some respect." The twins looked at her, stifled their giggles, and vanished behind a willow tree. Rider sighed.

"Let them be," Mokoya said. "They're only children."

They watched light dancing over her daughter's headstone. "Could you have imagined this," Rider said, "all those years ago, in the dust, when we first met?"

Mokoya laughed. "In those days, I tended not to imagine happy endings."

Rider squeezed her hand, where a symphony of reds was spreading upward. She returned the gentle pressure. But even as she did so, there was a sense of something not being *right,* like a dislocation between vision and reality.

Someone was tapping on her forehead.

Mokoya wrinkled her brows. There was warmth around her, and softness: a bed, padded with cotton, heated to the right temperature, the air sharp with cleansing herbs.

"Don't you think you've slept for long enough?"

Mokoya opened her eyes. Akeha's face hovered over hers, his expression arranged into one of fond disgust. She found her voice in a throat cracked and dry with disuse. "Akeha? What—what happened?"

"You're alive, even though you shouldn't be."

Mokoya blinked. Akeha spoke to someone off to the

side. "Go and fetch the Head Abbot at once." A patter of running feet.

As the calm of the graveyard receded from her—Vision? Dream?—the reality of the present flowed into place. She lay on a bed in a high-roofed room, royally appointed, the sheets brocaded and the bed drapes fine and rich. Silk screens, not paper, stood in window frames. Somewhere a bird sang.

"Don't try to sit up," he said.

She tried anyway, and something in her lower back twanged. She dropped onto the bed with a grunt. Memories filtered back to her, of the last fight with the naga, of her mortal wounding. She tried to move her feet, heavy under a blanket. One foot twitched awkwardly, then the other.

"You didn't lose any organs this time, if you're wondering."

"I thought I was dead."

"You were. Good as, anyway. Heart stopped, everything broken . . ."

"But, yet, somehow I survived."

"It's a good thing you made a new friend. I don't know what kind of Quarterlandish black magic they practice, but they managed to . . . stop you somehow. Stop? I don't know what that means. They tried to explain it, but it sounded like nonsense." He shrugged. "Anyway, they kept your spirit with us until we brought you back here."

"They're alive?"

Akeha receded to the post at the foot of the bed. "You'll be happy to hear that no one died in your little heroic scheme. Well, except for the naga. Couldn't have saved it anyway—it was too badly hurt."

"And the city?" she asked.

"Rebuilding. It'll take a while." He snorted. "Even with the help of Protectorate troops."

Mokoya tried sitting up again, and this time got as far as her elbows, where she stayed. "So Mother's troops are in the city?"

Akeha shrugged; he looked tired. Mokoya sighed.

A billow of ocher robes heralded Thennjay's arrival in the doorway. "Nao." He crossed the room rapidly as Mokoya pushed herself up to sitting, ignoring the protests made by her slowly healing body. Her left wrist hurt. Thennjay pulled her into a half embrace, his arm around her shoulders, pressing her head into the cloth of his belly. She inhaled, smelling incense and sweat as he sighed, a deep rumble through his bones.

"Why was I surprised to find that you'd run off to martyr yourself?" he said, when they broke from the embrace. He put a gentle hand on her cheek.

She leaned into his touch. "Where is everyone?"

"Everyone?" Akeha said. "Hmph. Phoenix is busy

frolicking with her new best friend. Adi and her crew are helping with reconstruction and annoying the wits out of my people. Or she's annoying *me,* at least. The raja and his daughter have been enjoying some *quality* family time."

"But that's not the question you're asking, is it?" Thennjay said.

She wet her lips and swallowed. "I want to see them," Mokoya said.

"Come." Thennjay held out an arm.

Akeha narrowed his eyes. "The doctor said her spine will take time to heal. Should she be walking around?"

Mokoya made a dismissive noise. She braced her weight with her arms and pushed her legs off the bed. They moved sluggishly and unevenly. Distinct lines of pain flared across her back and the muscles of her thighs. She was aware of bandages wrapped tight around her left leg, and her right ankle was encased in a solid, molded cast. She closed her eyes and examined her injuries through forest-nature. Healing bones, torn flesh slowly knitting whole. There were metal implants in her right ankle. Walking would be difficult.

She planted her feet on the cool stone floor, pressed her weight onto Thennjay's arm, and stood.

Thennjay looped one arm around her waist as pain threatened to fell her again. Mokoya pushed her own body upright through water-nature. Thennjay dissipated earth-nature from around them, lessening the weight of her body. "Lean on me," he said. "Don't put pressure on that ankle."

Akeha tutted as Thennjay led her into the first staggering step. Her legs were disobedient, unwilling to bend. "You suffered some nerve damage," Thennjay said. "Training your body to move properly again will take time."

"I'm going to get the doctor," Akeha said in disgust.

Thennjay grunted. "You know where to find us."

They made their way snail-paced through corridors, between the hanging tapestries of the raja's palace. Sound bubbled up from the city below, carrying with it a vivid jumble of emotions: happiness, anger, excitement, sadness. Life moving forward. Mokoya found that the pain was manageable, and the unevenness of her slow steps began to take on a regularity. The floor was solid beneath her. She was here. She was present.

"What will happen to the Machinists in Bataanar, now that Protectorate troops have moved in?" Mokoya asked.

"They've gone to ground for now," Thennjay said. "But I suspect this won't be the end of it. It's funny, you know. Raja Choonghey could have reported them. He had so much evidence on his hands."

"But he didn't. Why?"

"Maybe he saw their usefulness at last. After all, if not

for them, that night might have turned out very differently. Or maybe Akeha's words finally had an effect on him. Who knows?"

"I'm glad."

They shuffled on. Mokoya could feel a cramp building in her left calf, the one supporting the bulk of her weight. She said, "You know, if you just told me where they are, I could save us both a lot of trouble."

"Yes, but you need to get used to walking. You can't jump from place to place forever."

"Rider has jumped from place to place all their life. Walking is overrated."

Thennjay chuckled. "We spent a lot of time talking while you were asleep. They tried to teach me their trick, but I couldn't do it. You had an unfair advantage."

"You mean my prophet nature?"

"That's what they suspect. The way they explained it, there are also prophets among the Quarterlanders, but they are very rare. One in a hundred thousand, maybe fewer. Over there, they think of it as a curse. No mortal should be expected to control fortune, intentionally or not."

"It is a curse. I've never felt otherwise."

"Well, at least now we know it isn't a death sentence. Prophecies can be undone. That's more than we had before."

"I want to know if it's possible to stop them forever."

"We'll have time to find out." Thennjay gently squeezed her closer. "I like Rider. I'm glad you met them. You make a bright picture together."

Mokoya smiled. Her arm flushed warm and red, a mellow sort of joy.

"Almost there now." Thennjay gestured with his chin to a circular door ahead of them.

Within that room a zither was being indecorously and inexpertly played, a fierce joy extant in the dissonant twang of its strings. As the tangle of music drifted down the corridor Mokoya remembered golden, perfumed summer days in the Great High Palace, giggling as she learned the art from her mother's courtesans.

The doorway framed a wide, rosewood-toned room basking in the lucid glow of midday sunlight. In its middle, on a stack of yellow cushions, Princess Wanbeng and Rider sat in the company of a zither. The latter had their back to Mokoya, hunched over in concentration as their amateurish fingers skipped and stumbled through Wanbeng's instructions. Mokoya studied the earnest slope of their back and imagined the look on their face, brow creased in completely sincere focus. She rested against the curved edge of the doorway with a soft sigh. She could stay here indefinitely, watching and listening.

Wanbeng looked up briefly, and a small exclamation passed her lips. "Tensor!"

Rider turned around, startled. Then their eyes met, and in that moment Mokoya could not have cared less about the world around them, about woven fates and political desires and things that were left behind. In that moment, all that mattered was the halo of light around their head, the smile on their face, and the movement of their lips as they said one word:

"Mokoya."

# About the Author

Photograph by Nicholas Lee

**JY YANG** is a lapsed journalist, a former practicing scientist, and a master of hermitry. A queer, nonbinary, postcolonial intersectional feminist, they have over two dozen pieces of short fiction published in places including *Uncanny Magazine, Lightspeed, Strange Horizons,* and *Tor.com.* They live in Singapore, edit fiction at Epigram Books, and have a master's degree in creative writing from the University of East Anglia. Find out more about them and their work at jyyang.com, and follow them on Twitter: @halleluyang.

# TOR·COM

**Science fiction. Fantasy. The universe.**

**And related subjects.**

*

More than just a publisher's website, *Tor.com*
is a venue for **original fiction, comics,** and
**discussion** of the entire field of SF and fantasy,
in all media and from all sources. Visit our site
today—and join the conversation yourself.